Future Tense . . .

I saw movement out of the corner
of my eye.

She came out from behind my car
and she held a big Colt .45 in her hand
that pointed at me. I could have put my
finger on the place where the slug
would hit.

A .45 makes a hole on the way out
you can bury your fist in.

That movement was frozen forever
in my memory. Every cinder in the small
parking lot stood out and I could feel
the grain of the gray wooden railing
under my hand. She wore an aqua sun suit.
Her blonde hair was wild and tangled
and her face was puffy from weeping.

She stared up at me, foreshortened
by the height.

Her eyes were like broken stone.

"Stand still for it, you son-of-a-bitch,"
she said.

Also by John D. MacDonald:

All These Condemned   14239 $1.75
April Evil   14128 $1.75
Ballroom of the Skies   14143 $1.75
The Beach Girls   14081 $1.75
A Bullet for Cinderella   14106 $1.75
Clemmie   14015 $1.75
Condominium   23525 $2.25
Contrary Pleasure   14104 $1.75
The Crossroads   14033-4 $1.75
The Damned   13997 $1.50
Dead Low Tide   14166 $1.75
Deadly Welcome   13682 $1.50
Death Trap   13557 $1.50
The Deceivers   14016 $1.75
The Drowner   13582 $1.50
The End of the Night   14192 $1.75
End of the Tiger and Other Stories   14241 $1.75
The Executioners   14059 $1.75

The Brass Cupcake

JOHN D. MacDONALD

FAWCETT GOLD MEDAL • NEW YORK

THE BRASS CUPCAKE

Copyright © 1950 by John D. MacDonald

All rights reserved

Published by Fawcett Gold Medal Books, a unit of CBS
Publications, the Consumer Publishing Division of CBS Inc.

ISBN: 0-449-14141-1

Printed in the United States of America

27   26   25   24   23   22   21   20   19   18   17   16

1

On a day when the February sun is indiscriminately painting all shades, from cherry red to tobacco-spit brown, on the shapes draped across our beaches . . .

On a morning when the tanned young things are striding down the beach foam line with a hip-roll strut, and a broker from Chicago cackles, points, and nudges a banker from Seattle with his elbow, finally daring a meek whistle when the tanned young things are well out of earshot . . .

On a morning when you are at last positive that nothing has ever happened to you and now, at the advanced age of thirty-three, it is pretty evident that nothing ever will . . .

On a sun-split morning when the recumbent forms seem to crackle and spit under the yellow fist of the sun and you sit on the edge of your bed and scratch the sole of one bare foot with the toes of the other and belch without pleasure and rub your grainy eyes with your knuckles . . .

It picks that morning to happen.

Incorrect. It picks that morning for it to be discovered that it indeed happened the night before.

I sat there.

I woke up at ten. By then it was three hours old. At seven, precisely, one Frances Audrey, colored, let herself into the large second-floor water-front apartment rented by one Elizabeth Stegman of Boston, Massachusetts. The apartment was in something uncleverly called the Tide Winds on North Florence Beach, just outside Florence City, Florida.

Frances was all right until she peered around the edge of the open door into Miss Stegman's bedroom. . . .

5

I showered, dressed, and was out of my room—politely called an "efficiency apartment"—by ten-twenty. I was five steps down from my locked door when I heard my phone ring. I shrugged it off. The mood had been on me now, gathering force, for a year. You know the kind of mood. It slugged you on rainy days when you were a kid. Maybe you ran to Mother moaning, "I hate all my toys and myself too." Nobody could possibly be calling me that I had the faintest interest in talking to.

I breakfasted on coffee and walked the six slow blocks to the office. The Waggoner Block. Third floor. Air-conditioned. Security Theft and Accident Insurance Company, Inc. A. Myers—District Manager.

You go in the door into a sort of pigpen effect, three chairs for waiting with a fence around them, a swinging gate in the fence. At the right of the fence is the reception desk. Wilma Booton, a thin, sallow, rough-skinned blonde, handles the reception desk, the pocket-size switchboard, and the reports to the home office in Hartford with hyperthyroid efficiency. She looks, from throat to ankles, remarkably like a plucked turkey neck. Dead ahead, through the gate, is the office of A. Myers. To the left of his is my smaller, simpler layout, with the printing on the door saying, "Clifford C. Bartells—Adjustments." To the far right is the salesman's bull pen, adjoining the office of Andrew Hope Maybree, District Sales Manager.

Wilma Booton gave a loud sniff that distended one nostril. "You took your time getting in this morning."

I put both hands on her desk and leaned forward until my chin was above the space bar on her typewriter.

"At three this morning, Wilma, beloved, I was in Tampa getting a signature on a waiver."

Myers, a bloated waxy-white little man who, sitting or standing, seems to be working out some intricate steps in a dance routine, appeared in his office doorway and said, "Stop making faces, Cliff. Come in, come in. Quick."

That was when I began to smell it in the air.

I glanced over at Kathy. Her eyes were wide and excited. I followed Myers into his office and shut the door behind me. He stood, tap dancing, at the window, his back to me. "Sit down, Cliff. Sit down."

I sat, tapped a cigarette on the arm of the chair, and lit it.

He spun around and pointed a finger at me. A finger

like an uncooked enchilada. "You," he said, "are on the spot!"

"What have I been doing? Signing my own waivers?"

"Elizabeth Stegman is dead!"

"Well, fancy that! You know, Arthur, that is the last thing I thought you'd say. I can't get over it! And who is Liz?"

He went around his desk and sat down heartily. His feet kept tapping. "Who is *Liz?* Who *is* Liz?"

"Sorry. You're taking too long. Next contestant, please."

"For the love of God, Bartells, shut up!"

"When we adjusters get a union I won't have to take that sort of guff, boss."

"Forgive me. Forgive me. I'm excited. I'm sweating. Last night she was killed. Or maybe early this morning. The maid found her. I've been on the long-distance phone ever since, almost. She brought every piece of jewelry down with her. It's all gone. Every piece."

I was beginning to see the shape of things to come. "And we insured it, I suppose."

"For seven—hundred—and—fifty—thousand—dollars!"

No Moslem ever put more feeling into reading the Koran.

I took a deep and thoughtful drag on the cigarette. "And that, Arthur, is supposed to put me on the spot?"

At that moment his phone rang and he picked it up, hunched over it, his toes going tappety-tap under the desk. It gave me time to think of being on the spot before. Just a few years ago . . .

Florence City had grown amazingly fast while I was off to the wars. When I came back to my job on the Florence City police force, I found that with the growth had come a smear of big-city dirt. Inevitable, they said. You've got to play ball with one group of criminals, one syndicate, they said. That's the way to keep the city clean, they said. Treat 'em right and they'll do their mischief out of town.

That was the way everything congealed in one instant in time to put me on the big spot. I went down that January morning in 1947 after ten motor-court robberies and found the kid there. They had been beating him for a long time without ever marking him. The kid looked and moved like an old man. They'd got a confession out of him for the whole ten robberies. I talked to him in the cell, on a hunch, and I found out to my own satisfaction that the kid hadn't done a single one of them. So on the day they had it all set to put him away for five years I found out that it was one of the local boys who had got a little frisky and had paid off a percentage to the Chief to have the vagrant set up like a clay duck.

So I went to court and blew it wide open and three days later I was a patrolman, on foot. The only cop on foot in the whole city.

When you're a lieutenant, you get a gold badge in Florence City. Very fancy. Just enough blue enamel. Not too much. And then they took it away from me. But a funny thing happened. When they took it, it wasn't gold any longer. Just brass. The fact that they could take it away on a deal like that changed the metallic composition.

Once, as a kid on the bum, I was stuck in a county can in the coal-mine area of southern Illinois. They had their own language in that jail. Anything you got by guile— extra cigarettes, more food, a pint bottle—was called a cupcake. You could lose a cupcake the same way.

So when they took it away from me, it wasn't even a badge any more. Just another cupcake. Something I chiseled and then got chiseled out of. A brass cupcake. Something of no importance. No importance at all. Yet I cried into my pillow like a fool kid that night.

I resigned, of course, because that was what they expected. The process tagged me once and for all as a square cop—a Christer who couldn't be made.

It would have been easy to leave, and so I stayed. Security Theft and Accident decided that the cop background would make me a good adjuster. I handled cases for them and for other outfits not represented locally, on a fee basis. And it turned out that I was a natural middleman for the return of stolen property. I got a three-thousand bonus on one case by buying back forty thousand worth of emeralds for seventeen. On another case I made a five-thousand bonus by a cheap recovery of the merchandise on a policy that had a sixty-seven-thousand face value.

But slowly and surely I was going sour. I drank too much. I developed a wise line of chatter. Sure. I was Cliff Bartells, whose only stock in trade was an honesty that had backfired. And lately I realized that honesty for its own sake was beginning to lose its flavor. And that scared me.

Myers slapped the phone back into the cradle. He stared at me, almost absently. "What we've got to figure on, Cliff, is that whoever did it stayed right in town. I can't see any reason why they should run. You've got to get your lines out fast and find out if we can make a deal. I don't want that stuff fenced. I don't want it run out of the country."

"You make it sound simple."

"You've done it before."

"Let me ask one question. Do you think this will be kept out of the papers?"

"Are you crazy?"

"O.K. The lifeblood of this town is tourist dollars. Sure, the money from the groves adds up to something, but without dollars from Mr. Smith from points north, a lot of people go broke. I know what the pressure is on the force right now. All over the country people will read about the Stegman woman getting killed here by thieves. That isn't going to make anybody rush down this way, you know. Every civic organization, every businessman is going to be right on the back of the Commissioner's neck, and they won't let up until the front pages of every paper that carried the death carries an account of the arrest and conviction of the man or men who did it."

"I'm not so sure I follow you, Cliff."

"It's simple. Nobody will make a deal with me. Nobody will take that chance. The police will check every move I make. If I *should* be lucky and buy back the stones, they'll lock me up and they'll trample me until I tell who I made the deal with. If I don't talk, I'll stay in there until I come out tripping on my long white beard. And don't think Commissioner Guilfarr wouldn't enjoy it. He got real tired of me a few years back, you might remember."

"O.K., suppose you make the purchase and then talk."

"If I do, it's the last purchase I ever make. You know that. From then on my value on recoveries is nil. Word gets around fast these days. Nobody would ever deal with me again."

"They didn't make trouble the other two times, Cliff."

"Because nobody got killed and the thefts didn't get anything except local coverage, and not much of that. Deal me out of this one, Arthur."

"You can't do this to me!" he yelped.

"I want no part of it."

He scrubbed his forehead with his knuckles. "Cliff, kindly go into your office and wait while I make another call."

I went into my own office. Andrew Hope Maybree followed me in. He is tall with crisp chestnut hair, eyeglass lenses that always look highly polished, large yellow squirrel teeth in front and a fixed rule about always wearing a necktie even in the drugged heat of Florence City summer.

He seems to get a delicious sense of sin out of knowing me and being able to talk to me. I am a glamorous character to Andrew Maybree. An ex-cop. One who deals with the criminal element. He is so eager about it that I often find myself talking like something out of Hammett when he's around.

"Something big, hey, Cliff?"

"Murder for profit. The commonest kind."

"Will they get 'em? Will they?"

"Depends. If it was an amateur job, they probably will. If it was a pro job, they probably won't."

"Which was it, Cliff?"

"I'll tell you that after I find out how the woman died." Kathy appeared in the doorway. "He wants you now."

Again I sat down across the desk from Arthur. His feet tapped away on the asphalt tile floor. "I have . . . uh . . . explained your position to the home office, Cliff. And we . . . uh . . . see eye to eye on what to do about it. The home office is worried because none of the stones are really distinctive. They can all be pried out of the settings and fenced quite safely. They agree that I can't order you to go ahead and try to make a recovery. You'd be well within your rights to refuse. And they can see that the amount we pay would have to be generous before the people who did this thing will want to deal with you. So they're transferring three hundred thousand to our account here. That's the top you can offer them. If you can swing it successfully, the company will give you a bonus of . . . uh . . . thirty thousand."

I met his glance. His eyes wavered and slid away. Old Myers, trying to save money for the company. It's hard for him to buy a nickel pack of gum without trying to get it for four cents.

"Call them back," I said. "Tell them it has to be fifty."

"That's a large amount," he complained.

"So is a seven-hundred-and-fifty-thousand-dollar loss. And it's obvious that the stones are worth more than the face value of the policy, or they wouldn't go as high as three hundred."

"All right," he said. "Forty thousand." I shook my head. "Forty-five?" I smiled at him. "Fifty, fifty, fifty," he said, irritated. "Fifty thousand dollars. They are thieves and murderers. You're a bandit."

"Payable ten a year for five years. And I want it in writing and I want your signature on it and I want Kathy to notarize it."

"All right, all right!" he snapped. He leaned back and the swivel chair creaked. For a moment his restless feet were stilled.

"Send Kathy in and I'll dictate the agreement."

Fifteen minutes later I heard the busy clack of Kathy's typewriter stop, heard the quick tap, tap, tap of her heels as she came into my office. She came around behind the desk and laid the unsigned agreement in duplicate in front of me. "See if it's O.K. before I take it in for signature, huh?"

She was beside me, the scent of her around me, pressing warmly against my shoulder. Kathy is a slight brunette, deeply tanned. She gives the impression of not having enough skin to fit her comfortably, so that it's stretched tight over every inch of her, giving a tilt to her dark eyes, shortening her moist upper lip, giving the rest of her an exciting and pneumatic piquancy. Andrew Hope Maybree and I have been dating her from time to time. It's too much to see that walking around the office each day.

I know that Andrew, by his puzzled expression when he looks at her, has found out the same thing I have. First base can be made. You can get to second with a hook slide. But no matter how hard you try to round third, you get tagged out with enough vigor to cross your eyes. She is warm and young and well fashioned, but invulnerable.

The reason is quite simple: Kathy wants to be married. She bends over children with little warm cries in her throat. She presses her nose against furniture-store windows.

Her warm breath touched my ear lobe. "Aren't you the one!" she whispered.

"It looks nice in print, eh?"

"I broke the point on the pencil when he named the figure, Cliff. He said it as though the words were strangling him."

"There was somebody," I said, "a long time ago. They killed him by pouring molten gold down his throat."

"You know a thousand little things and you never can remember the names, darling. Besides, Arthur wasn't swallowing. He was coughing up. In his little heart Arthur owns all of the company. Every share of stock."

"When someday they tie the can to him it should come as a great blow. And would you please ease off on the gentle pressure against my shoulder, love?"

She moved away quickly, snatched up the papers, and made a face at me. She headed out of the office, her heels going clack, clack, the firm taut little haunches clenching under the close-fitting skirt. She went out under full sail, using the after deck, the fantail, as a medium of expression. With it she said, "Nuts!" Firmly.

She was back in three minutes with the original for me, signed and impressed with her notary seal. Again she came around the desk when it would have been far simpler to slide it across to me. Her fingers touched lightly against the nape of my neck.

"I haven't seen you in ever and ever so long, Cliff," she murmured.

"Gee, and now I've got a dowry, too," I said.

Her lingering fingers stiffened and she slapped the back of my head before she went back around the desk. "You stink, Bartells," she said, her eyes narrowed.

I laughed at her until her anger faded. She grinned and left. She resents having her secret shared. She resents having anyone look into her mind and see cottage, curtains, play pens, sand piles, and a big milk bill.

I mailed the agreement to myself, turned over my office and the routine stuff to Mart Powers, and informed Arthur I was off on a leave of absence. He stood up and tap-danced me out to the gate. Wilma stared at me with venomous eyes. Decent people work from nine to five. Wilma's brand of decent people. I saw her one Christmas wistfully eying an apple-cheeked Salvation Army lad outside the post office. Hosts of angels were in Wilma's eyes. Then she saw me grinning at her. She turned valentine red and has hated me ever since.

Florence City met the hot February sun with a wide financial smile. The cars of an estimated seventy thousand tourists edged through the choked streets. Florence City lay under the sun like a sleepy nude under a G.E. lamp.

Before the war Florence City was a quiet middle-class resort. But the war expanded the field of endeavor. Gambling houses, breast of guinea hen under glass, seagoing yachts from Havana, seventy-dollar night-club tabs for a quiet dinner for two—with the appropriate wines, of course. The bakers from Dayton and the shoe clerks from Buffalo still came down, but the high rentals had shoved them inland off the beaches, in as far as the swamps and the mangroves and the orange-juice factories.

A new group had taken over the beaches. Middle-aged ladies with puffy faces and granite eyes brought down whole stables of hundred-dollar call girls, giggling like a sorority on a social welfare trip. But the rate was bumped to two hundred to cover the higher cost of accommodations and the traveling expenses. Sleek little men with hand-blocked sport shirts strolled around and made with the Bogart gestures.

Boom town, fun town, money town, rough town. Lay it on the line. You can't take it with you. Next year comes the H bomb. Put it on the entertainment account.

I stood near the office and watched them. The haltered girls, the bald lobster-pink heads, the big convertibles. You could look into a pair of eyes and tell at once if the owner was a local or a tourist. Local eyes held a wearied acceptance. Tourist eyes had a bright glaze, a hectic promise, a threat of excitement.

As I walked toward the parking lot to get my car, I saw my reflection in a store window, saw it before I had prepared myself to see it, and thus achieved for one small moment a bitter objectivity.

I saw the heavy slabs of the shoulders, the hooded and secretive eyes, the black hair thinning back at the tem-

ples, the somber, almost petulant cast of the mouth. A big
man. A big stranger with rocks in his fists and broken
dreams swinging from the angles of his heart and a gray
nausea in his brain.

Mom, it's raining out and I hate my toys and I hate
myself too.

"Run along and play."

Aw . . .

"Run along and play like a nice little boy. Go find the
pretty stones, darling. Then we'll give you fifty thousand
dollars and you can buy ten thousand fifths of bourbon,
or ten pretty automobiles, or just dozens and dozens of
playmates, or maybe a little of all three."

Gee!

"But son! Be careful you don't get your head stomped
in."

The inside of the car was an oven. The sweat rolled
into my eyes, stinging, before I could get the crate rolling.

2

SERGEANT BANSON lives with his two kids and his sister
in a white clapboard four-room house on a fifty-by-eighty
lot east of town where the mosquitoes come big and come
hungry, like knives in the night.

It could be a house in Portland or Columbus or Stevens
Point, Wisconsin—except for the sandy yard, the jaca-
randa tree, the acacia tree, the small, dusty, discouraged
palm.

Washing hung on the back-yard line. Big red ants were
carrying on extensive engineering operations near the
garbage can.

I rattled the screen door of the kitchen and the Sergeant's sister waddled to the door and stared at me with
frank animosity. "You shouldn't come here," she said. I
could tell from the way she pitched her voice that Harry
was home and asleep.

"I want to talk to him."

"He needs his sleep bad. Why do you keep bothering
him?"

"Let's let Harry decide whether he wants to talk to
me, shall we?"

"I'm not going to wake him up for you."

"Then I'm coming in and wake him up myself." I pushed the door open. She didn't object. She waddled back over to the sink, sniffing audibly.

Harry was in the front bedroom. The shades were drawn. Coming out of the sunlight like that, it took quite a time for my eyes to get used to the dimness. Harry's rattling snore seemed to catch in his throat each time, then burst forth with a gluey sound. He was naked except for underwear shorts. His long, yellowish body was stringy and lean except for the hard mound of the belly. He was plagued with bad teeth and the smell of his breath was in the room. The holstered .38 was hung over the back of the chair.

I lit a cigarette and sat on the edge of the bed. I grabbed his knee and shook him. His flesh was warm and sticky. "Wake up, Harry. Wake up."

He mumbled, then sat bolt upright with a great gasp, his hand reaching over for the revolver. His eyes were wide and staring.

"Wha' . . . Oh, you," he said. He yawned. I lit another cigarette off mine and handed it to him. He took it and his eyes had turned snake-hard. "What the hell are you doing here, Cliff?"

"Don't hemorrhage, Harry. I left the car over on the highway and came in the back."

A complaining tone crept into his voice. "I don't know what you got to bother me about, Cliff. You know if people talk about you coming here it eight-balls me with the Chief and the Commissioner."

"If you don't tell 'em, they won't know. You're off duty. I'm just a friend."

"Great friend!"

"I'm on this Stegman deal."

His eyes widened. "Lord Mabel!"

"Just give me a review, Harry."

"You musta gone nuts, Bartells. They're itching for you to step into this kind of mess. The Commissioner'll bust you wide open right down the middle." He coughed. "You got no more chance of buying that ice back than you have of flying like a big bird. If they ever find out you're interested, they'll dream up something to charge you with."

"Just what happened, Harry?"

"It'll be in the afternoon paper, Cliff."

"I want you to tell me."

"And you can go to hell," he said gruffly.

I snapped my cigarette at the far wall. It hit under a framed photograph of Angela and the two kids. We both watched the sparks shower down and glimmer out against the rug and the wooden floor.

"And just how is Angela?" I asked gently.

Just before the war Harry Banson, then a bachelor of forty, went down into the swamps to pick up a suspect. The suspect had a cousin named Angela—a doughy, smiling little girl of sixteen. Harry brought them both back. He jailed the suspect and married Angela, the little swamp rabbit. She had three kids in three years. One died. Her lungs went bad. They got so bad that the force stopped kidding Harry about his swamp rabbit. I, as lieutenant, rearranged the roster so as to put Harry in the way of two fat rewards. With those rewards he managed to send Angela out to Denver to give her lungs a chance to heal.

"Angela's a lot better, damn you."

I stood up. "Did I ever lever you with that before? Did I? Banson, you can keep that mouth of yours shut and you can go to hell too."

He leaned over the edge of the bed and butted his cigarette against the floor.

"Sit down, then," he said with a weary tone. "But you're plain crazy to stick your nose into this. The way they're acting down there, if they don't find the somebody who did it pretty soon, they'll pick up somebody and yank out a confession."

I sat back on the bed. "We got the call at five after seven this morning," he said. "Her name was Elizabeth Stegman and she was fifty-nine years old. She came from Boston in a big new Buick with her personal maid and her chauffeur. They got here January third. The maid and the chauffeur are man and wife. She got them a place in town where they could keep the car under cover. She took over a nine-hundred-a-month apartment out at the new place, the Tide Winds. The apartment has a big bedroom, sun deck, living room with the wall facing the ocean all glass front, kitchen, and all done real nice.

"The chauffeur has a license to carry a gun on account of this Elizabeth Stegman—a spinster, by the way—trucks all her jewelry down here with her. She puts it in the Florence City Bank until the landlord can have one of those little barrel safes put in the apartment at her expense. Every day is the same, the chauffeur and maid say. Their names are Franklin, Horace and Letty Franklin, and they live in the Belle-Anne Courts out on Bay Drive. A Nigra girl named Frances Audrey sneaks in about seven and cleans up all the apartment except the bedroom. She's hired to do that sort of work by this Lew Roma who owns the Tide Winds. Then about nine Horace and Letty come over. They've already had breakfast. Horace wakes her up, then cooks her breakfast while Letty gets the old lady dressed. While Horace serves her on the sun deck, Letty cleans up the bedroom. Every morning the same routine.

"But this morning Frances sees the bedroom door is open. The outside door was latched as usual, so Frances had to use her key. Frances looks in and there is the old doll in her pajamas on her face on the floor ten feet from the bed. She is under the safe, the safe door open, the picture that covered it thrown aside. The way it looks, somebody told her to use the combination to open the safe or else. And the moment the door swung open they bashed her behind the ear with a sap, using a full arm swing so that it busted the bone back of the ear like a clam shell and drove the splinters way into her brain.

"We are there ten minutes later. Nobody heard anything. Each upstairs apartment has a private stairway, so anybody could have gone up and knocked without being seen. The doc arrives and sets the time of death between midnight and two in the morning. Lew Roma tells us that some of the other residents were having noisy parties at about that time. The prints on the round safe door belong to the old lady. The door wasn't forced. No other prints that mean anything. All in all, a very professional job, Cliff, except for knocking the old lady off."

"What line are they taking downtown?"

"They gave the Franklins a very bad time, but it turns out Horace and Letty are in the clear. The Belle-Anne Courts is maybe three blocks from that little beer joint on Bay Drive called the Bomb Run. Horace and Letty have taken up table shuffleboard in a big way. There was a tournament there last night. The Franklins left at about quarter after two and they were there every minute. Fact is, they took second in the final play-offs. The last I

know, Letty Franklin tells the Chief that a niece of Miss
Stegman's, her only close relative and the girl who in-
herits, has been in town for two weeks, living at the Coral
Strand instead of with the old lady. I was dead for sleep
and I went off duty as the Chief was sending Buzz out to
pick her up."

"You know her name?"

He gave me a broken-toothed grin. "Hold on tight,
Cliff. The name is Melody Chance."

"Nobody has a name like that, unless they changed it
from Heimenpfeffer," I said.

"Now you know everything I know, Cliff," Harry
said. "I'm dead for sleep."

He lay back as I stood up and moved to the doorway.
He had his hands locked behind his graying head. "Watch
yourself, Cliff. Watch yourself."

His sister snorted as I went back through the kitchen.
I banged the screen door and cut across the sandy yard.
The littlest kid was standing by the sagging garage, towheaded, streaky-faced, three fingers in his mouth. He had
that wary swamp look around his eyes. It hadn't been
there when Angela had been around.

I drove slowly back into the traffic snarl. My "efficiency apartment" is over a Western Auto store two
blocks from the railroad station. I have a private parking
space out behind the store. An outside open staircase,
spiked to the cinder blocks, leads up to my door. There
is another inside staircase that I seldom use.

I draped myself across the studio couch, set the phone
base on my chest, and dialed the Kit-Kat. When I went
to the wars there was no Kit-Kat. In fact, there was no
land where it stood. They made a fill for it, sucking up
the bay bottom and making a point of land into the bay
with the Kit-Kat at the end of it. By day it's a huge, low
L-shaped building in pastel pink, the L enclosing two
sides of a huge pool. A guard, stationed at the mainland
end, opens an impressive gate to let you into the parking
area. The short base of the L contains Tony Lavery's
offices and living quarters, as well as the biggest high-
limit gambling layout for a hundred miles around. The
long stem of the L contains bars, dining rooms, dance
floors, dressing rooms, and so on.

"Kit-Kat," a warm girl-voice said. "May we take your
reservation?"

"Is Tony in his office yet?"

"Just a moment, sir. I'll see if he's in. Who's calling?"

"Tell him it's the Clown Prince and see what he says."

The phrase was full of hoarse laughter. Languid Tony, surprisingly blond, had sent for me once, about a month after I exchanged my olive drab for police-force blue. Chief Powy told me I had to go. I'll never forget Tony's amused smile at my red, angry face. He slouched in his big office chair and said, "Baby, this is the new deal. Things have changed since you've been away, my buddee. In this pocket I got the Chief. Over here in this pocket I got the Commissioner. That's my job. I'm just the local errand boy for the syndicate. Between the three of us we keep the town nice and clean for the rabble. Right now you're a big hero. A prince of a fellow. But, baby, we'll make you a clown prince if you go Christer on us. We want you to be a good cop, but there are certain little local ordinances that you'd better ignore, the way we're ignoring them."

The girl was back on the line. "He'll take the call, sir. Just a moment."

"So it's you, baby," he said softly. "Don't tell me. Let me guess. Only you could be this dumb. Better take a run out here, if it's what I think it is."

"It is," I said. He told me to make it fast and hung up.

Palms were black paper cutouts against red fire in the western sky as I drove through the gates. The cocktail hour was well under way and there were about sixty cars in the big lot. I could hear people laughing out by the pool. When dusk approaches there is a new note in the laughter of women, as though the coming of night awakens something primitive, something that is buried deep when the sun is high.

The Kreshak twins met me outside Tony's office. They are beach boys. Tight silver trunks all day, nut-brown muscles like a Charles Atlas ad, at night they don beautifully tailored white jackets and take over the bouncing job. They're smooth at it. The noisy drunk suddenly sobers when the Kreshaks move in from either side and take hold of his arms in what looks, from ten feet away, like affection. Only the drunk knows that both hands have suddenly gone numb and the pain is curling his toes. They smile and make small talk and walk him quickly out.

I can't tell them apart. One said, "Do you smell cop?"

"The odor is faint. Maybe it's an ex-cop, Larry."

"Don't get me laughing," I said. "I become helpless."

"You ticklish, too?" Larry asked. He patted me quickly and lightly on all the possible places and said, "Oh, fudge! Nothing for my collection."

I looked at them closely. "Boys, I never noticed it before, but aren't you both getting a little bald?" Their color faded. "And a little thicker around the waist? You know what happens to aging beach boys. They end up looking like Dutch bartenders."

"Wise," Larry spat. "Wise."

"Tut, tut," I said. "Remember that all is vanity. It just seems a shame to see you boys going downhill so fast."

I went on into Tony's office. He was bending over a mirror laid flat on his desk, carefully clipping his small blond mustache. He glanced up. "Go make yourself a drink over in the corner, baby. With an Irish and water for me, no ice."

He slid the mirror and the scissors into the top desk drawer as I brought him his drink. I took my bourbon and soda over to the chair by the windows that looked out over the bay. A fishing launch was coming in late, running lights haloed by the evening mist rising off the water.

"I always gave you a mark for bright, baby," he said. "Now I wonder."

"I can try to buy, can't I?"

"Let me give it to you straight. Suppose I found out it was one of my boys. Just suppose. Or even three of my boys. My best boys. I'd have their bare feet heated up until I got the ice and a confession. And then I would turn them and the ice and the confession over to the law so fast it would make your head spin. That's how much I like this. Sure, I steered you into a contact on a couple of other deals. This is different. This is everybody's bread and butter, baby."

"How about rumors?"

"This big jewel stuff is different. The top boys have no crowd. They go it alone. Sometimes just a guy, singleton, or a couple. They dress the best, have the right cover stories, and lead clean and simple lives. With the mob that floods in here during the season, there could be a few strangers among us. I wouldn't know."

"Suppose you got a chance to make a contact?"

"I'd cross them, baby. I'd throw them to the law." He took out a nail file and began to work on his left thumbnail, tapering it to a smooth oval.

"I'm still buying," I said. "Three hundred packages of C notes, if anybody should mention it."

He whistled soundlessly. "It makes my mouth water. But not enough. A fix is a delicate thing. You know, if the law should get a line that it was one of my boys, my fix here wouldn't be worth a rusty fishhook. They'd stomp in and cream this whole operation. It's that big. And the syndicate would turn away and leave me for lost. I'm not fool enough to have any of this deal. And that's where I look at you—as the books say—askance. If my fix is no good, where would you stand if they found out down at the station that you happen to be in contact with the person who clobbered the old girl? I wouldn't want your bill for dental work. And if you never peeped, I bet they could stick you away for five without half trying. Withholding evidence of a murder. Something like that."

"There's another side to it, Tony."

He raised one delicately arched blond eyebrow. "Already I can see that. If you make it your business to cross them in order to make a big score for your company, what are you going to do for a job? Pick oranges?"

"It's clean healthy work."

"Now just suppose I was the guy who did it to the old girl. I put myself in his place. I'm so hot that probably the best thing I can do is stay right here. I want to unload the ice. What do I do? I handle it just like a snatch payoff. The ransom for Junior. Put dirty old bills in a shoebox and run like hell, I'd tell you. Then you've nothing to feed the cops."

"Maybe," I said.

He sighed and threw the nail file into the drawer. "A thing like this makes me nervous, baby. We are all munching on a nice big peaceful healthy pie and some creep has to throw a dead fish into the middle of it. We play for the big-money boys and girls. There are towns in the country where they feel safe because they know everything is under control. Up until today this was that kind of town. Word gets around. This has been a place for the happy Big Rich to kick up their heels. If all this hits them wrong, if the lid is slapped back on quick and tight, we'll be getting nothing but the Little Big Rich. The Big Rich tip a dime, wear a tweed suit for seven years, have their shoes resoled until there's no more uppers left. The Little Big Rich tip with the big bills, and wear a fortune on their backs. But in the pinch, when the little ball goes round and round and the bets are down, it's the little guy in the wrinkled tweed suit who is betting the house limit every time and who arrived in a hundred and sixty feet of boat worth five thousand a foot."

"I bleed for you," I said.

He smiled in a silky way. "Good-by, baby. You'll be bleeding another way soon enough. I got a friend who maybe'll let you help pick his oranges."

3

THE CORAL STRAND—"Apartments for Vacation Living"—looked like a place where guests at the Tide Winds might leave their pets.

It had been put up during the boom of the twenties, and at that time it had undoubtedly been bay-front property. But the lawyers couldn't have been so good. The bay at that point had been filled in until the Coral Strand was a good two hundred feet from the water, and the view was blocked off by a mammoth raspberry-colored project of more recent origin.

Once upon a time the Coral Strand, with its white stippled finish, must have looked like a bride's cake. Now it looked like a dirty shoebox that had been crumpled and straightened out again. It was even devoid of neon, an oversight in Florida amounting to heresy.

There was a wattled woman in the tiny office. She sat Buddha-like, amid a stench of mildew and rotting linoleum. She looked as though she had been a plump, jolly Mrs. Santa modeled out of wax, and then set too carelessly near a stove so that the wax had sagged.

"You wanna room we're full up."

"What room does Miss Chance have?"

"She ain't in."

"Maybe you didn't hear the question."

"You wanner, she's gone over to the public beach. Anyway, she said she was going there when she left here at ten o'clock this morning, maybe an hour ago. A fine thing I call it, her aunt layin' dead and her prancing around in that naked swimming suit she's got on. It ain't decent. Any decent girl'd be sittin' with her aunt and wearin' black insteada whorin' around town."

"I don't know her, but I want to go over to the public beach and look for her. What does she look like?"

"Who are you?"

I stared at her. She flushed and finally said, "All right. She's got a gray Chevvy business coupé with Massachusetts plates. She's wearin' a yella two-piece suit and a short yella coat. She's tallish and wears her hair long and it's a sorta silvery yella color. She's gotta snotty go-to-hell look."

"Was she in the other night when her aunt got killed?"

"Her!" the woman sneered. "Likely. She comes in three-four o'clock every night, for the whole two weeks she's been here. She gets out and I can rent to decent people."

I'd had about all I could take of her and the smell of that place.

"You've been too nice," I said.

The public beach was what you would expect of public beaches. A couple of hundred square inches of one's unclad beloved is charming. But when human hide comes in measurements of square acres, 99 per cent of it far from attractive, it is a bit overwhelming. Like the little French boy who lived in the forest and came home to find Mamma and Papa and his thirteen brothers and sisters all dead of eating poisoned mushrooms. For the death of any one of them he would have wept his heart out. But to see all fifteen of them there made a fantastic farce of death, and the little French boy laughed and laughed and laughed.

I stood by the parked cars and looked down across the slope of sand and flesh and gay colors. In thirty seconds I saw fourteen tall blonde girls in yellow suits. So I went back to the gray Chevvy with the Massachusetts plates. It was unlocked and the windows were rolled down.

We are prone to forget that a car is as responsive to its owner and to his personality as a pet would be. I slid behind the wheel. Sherlock Bartells. The seat was far enough back to prove she was long-legged. A yellow thread on the seat proved that I probably had the right car.

The cigarette butts in the ash tray had smudges of red-orange lipstick, a shade that would suit a dark-skinned blonde. There was enough sand on the floor boards to show that she came to the beach often. The wear on the pedals showed that she rode the clutch too much. By finding where the rear-vision mirror was focused, I checked her dimensions even further. A short-waisted, long-legged blonde. I found a long silvery-blonde hair on the seat back. I pulled it through my fingernails and it coiled into a tiny perfect spring. A healthy blonde.

Feeling pleasantly fatuous, I went back onto the beach. I narrowed the fourteen down to three. I stepped around the prone bodies. Closer inspection narrowed the three down to two. A small brown creature came rocketing up to one of the two, yelling, "Mommy, Mommy, Mommy!" And then there was one.

I sat on my heels beside her. She was on her face on a dark blue blanket, her head turned away from me. Wide slim shoulders tapered down to a small waist and tender concavity before the convex flaring curve of hip. The hand at the end of her long, round, brown arm had a square, stubborn, childish look. You have your superstitions; I'll keep mine. Long-fingered women are feline. Stubby-fingered women with square hands are open and eager and frank.

She must have felt someone near her. She rolled away from me, onto her side, propped up on her right elbow. A sheaf of the long ripe-wheat hair was across her face and she threw it back with a quick motion of her head. "You wouldn't be nearsighted," she said. Her voice was low and husky-hoarse, the kind of voice that Bankhead and Dietrich have. In it was a thin trace of finishing schools and Beacon Hill. Her face was a long oval, with good and well-pronounced bone structure of brow. The mouth was hers alone. The lip shape had that odd squareness which looks harsh and bold. But at the same time it hinted of vulnerability. The sun glare had diminished the pupils of her eyes, and their smallness emphasized the shifting gray-green of the irises.

"I wish," I said, "I had a nice infallible line. Something that would work good. Then you wouldn't even have to be Melody Chance."

"Why don't you take a nice long walk down the beach? Go feed the sea gulls."

"I'm a citizen with business to transact. I want to discuss the policy on Aunt Elizabeth's jewels."

"You can still take that walk."

We glared at each other. Sweat was running down my chest under my shirt. Defiance was shining bright in her large eyes.

"It's a hell of a lot easier for an ugly woman to be pleasant," I snapped.

"Meaning?"

"You're all carried away with yourself."

"When I want a personality course, friend, I'll go to somebody who hasn't got a mad on at the world."

"I never found anybody so remarkably easy to dislike, Miss Chance."

"All you need . . ."

"I'll decide what I need, and . . ."

"Oh, shut up!"

I wanted to throw a handful of sand in her face. We kept glaring. The corners of her mouth twitched. I felt the laughter coming up in my throat. I fought to keep it back. Then, like two fools, we were grinning at each other.

"Maybe it's the heat," I said.

She stood up. "We can't talk here. You take the blanket. I'll get the other stuff."

I shook the blanket out and folded it. She walked ahead of me up to her car. Her carriage was like that of the Mexican women, all movement from the waist down, head high, shoulders squared, hip-tilt in the direction of each limber stride.

At the car she put her things on the front seat and turned to face me. I had been trying to decide about her.

"I was going to make noises like an insurance man," I said, "and make a point of not trusting you any further than absolutely necessary. Now I've got a new angle."

"People who want to trust me make me suspicious."

"Stay suspicious. It'll be healthy. Have you got plans for tonight?"

"Let's not try to parlay this insurance deal into a lonely-hearts project."

"Damnit, drop your guard for a minute. If I feel like making a pass later on, you can apply the brush, but give me a chance to do my job first."

"So I'm free tonight." The hostility faded suddenly

and her face was empty. An almost frightening emptiness. As though nothing in this world could ever touch her again.

"I know where you live. Be out on the curb at six-fifteen. Light dress and some kind of jacket, because it may get cold later on."

By the time I had got into my car she was already headed back for the beach, carrying the blanket.

A harelipped young man in a shirt decorated with tropical fish told me that the Franklins were in Number 8, and he thought they were both in. Eight was around in the back.

Horace Franklin, it turned out, was the man in bathing trunks washing a big long black Buick in front of Number 8. His shoulders were sunburned and his torso was hairless, smoothly muscled. His black hair had a gleam like the Buick. His face was a smooth expressionless oval and his eyelids were so heavy that they gave him a slightly sinister look, a hooded, watchful look. Faces mean nothing. I found that out once when we brought in a guy who had killed three small children for laughs. He was the nearest thing to Van Johnson I ever saw. When he smiled his eyes danced. And he had a deep, warm laugh.

This Horace Franklin looked at my card without taking it. He turned off the hose, wrung out the sponge, and laid it carefully on top of the car. The screen door slapped as his wife, Letty, came out of the court apartment. She wore a pale blue bare-midriff sun suit. She was a stocky, hard-muscled blonde with thick thighs, big firm breasts, and a flat-footed stance. Without the long, thin, high-bridged nose she could have been attractive.

"What does he want, Horace?" She slurred the word so that it sounded as though she were calling him Horse.

"From the insurance company. The one insured the jewelry. Name's Bartells."

"This stinkin' town," Letty said. "Jesus, this stinkin' town. Mr. Bartells, when that lawyer gets down here you tell him that we demand transportation back to Boston and a letter of reference."

"Shut up and get in the house," Horace said tonelessly.

"If you don't mind, Mr. Franklin, I'd like to have your wife included when I ask these questions."

He smiled tautly. "Maybe we're sick of answering questions, Mister."

"I know that you're being given a bad time. This was a most unfortunate thing."

"Hah!" he said.

"Under the terms of the policy," I said, "Miss Stegman agreed to use reasonable care in protecting the insured gems from theft."

"Hell," said Horace, "I would have thought it was easier to get gold out of Fort Knox than it'd be to . . ."

"Horace!" Letty said sharply. We both turned and looked at her. The end of her pointed nose quivered. She moved out toward me and lowered her voice. "You work for a living like we do, don't you? All the old lady did was clip coupons. She was loaded. And it all goes to that night-club tramp, doesn't it?"

"What are you getting at?" I asked, knowing well what was in her mind.

"Maybe we can't remember so good. Maybe the old lady was so careless with that stuff we had to go along behind her picking it up. Maybe she never locked the safe at night. Would you people still pay off?"

"That's hard to say, isn't it? The executor of the estate could probably find some of her friends who'd be willing to swear that she used reasonable care."

"He might not want to go to all that trouble," she said, smiling.

There was plenty of larceny in her heart. Horace looked moodily at her. "Shut up," he said.

She leaned toward him, her hands on her hips. "Listen to you, and I spend the rest of my life doing somebody else's housework. You're a real smart one, you are."

His palm bounced off the side of her face. She staggered heavily. He followed her up, backhanded her across the mouth, turned her around, and pushed her toward the door. She trudged in meekly like a punished child and the door slapped shut behind her. I could barely hear the thin noises she was making.

Horace looked mildly at the back of his hand. He wiped it on his swimming trunks. "Miss Stegman was a fine woman to work for. We've both been with her for nearly six years now. She was careful about the jewelry.

Mrs. Franklin is pretty broken up over all this. She doesn't know what she's saying."

"It seems funny to me that Miss Stegman wouldn't have rented a place that had servants' quarters adjoining it."

"It troubled her, sir, that she couldn't locate such a place. But this arrangement worked out very nicely."

"Up until night before last."

His lips tightened. "Yes, sir. Up until the night before last."

"It leaves you in an unfortunate position, doesn't it?"

He shrugged. "We're dependent on Miss Chance. I took the liberty of consulting a lawyer this morning. He advised me to stay right here. We have wages coming, of course, but her obligation to send us back home is moral rather than legal. We hope that Miss Stegman's lawyers will advance money to Miss Chance in anticipation of her inheritance so that she can . . . provide for us."

"The inheritance is large?"

His tongue flicked across his underlip. "Quite large, I believe. There's the big house at Dedham, of course, and the summer house at the Cape, and then she always seemed to have an ample income for everything. She was . . . generous with us. That's not counting the jewelry, of course. I should say, the insurance money for the jewelry."

I watched him closely as I said, "Oh, I think we'll make a hundred-per-cent recovery on the insured items."

One eyebrow went up. "What's that?"

"We generally buy the items back from the thief. If not, we either replace the jewelry in kind or pay off on the policy, whichever is cheaper. We're paying the sum of four hundred thousand for the jewelry."

He glanced toward the door and then back at me. "You've made a contact?"

"We will soon. We always do." I smiled. "Naturally, this is confidential information."

"Naturally," he said.

"You see," I said, "it's good business for us to offer more than a fence would offer. It cuts our potential loss quite a lot."

"I see."

"I suppose Miss Stegman was on good terms with her niece?"

He glanced sharply at me. The corners of his mouth turned down. "I wouldn't say that."

"If I get a chance I'll put in a word for you with Miss Chance."

"We'll appreciate it."

Before I rounded the corner I glanced back. He stood with the sponge in his hand, kneading it in his strong-looking fingers, looking off into the distance. I slowed down as I approached my car. A prowl car was hemming it in, angled sharply across my bows.

Chief Powy stood nibbling on a kitchen match. He's a butter-soft hulk of a man with a frog voice, tombstone teeth, and little, vague, wandering eyes. Gilman and De Rider, both in gray uniform, stood near him.

Chief Powy nodded at them. Gilman and De Rider are Powy's pets. They're so much of a type that they look related. Big and heavy and young, with leather faces and faded blue eyes and brutal mouths. Southern storm troopers.

I walked into it. There wasn't anything else to do. They enjoyed their work. Locally, it's called "the rough search." The idea is ostensibly to frisk a man for weapons, but to do it in such a way that you rumple and tear his clothes and jar him up a little with the heel of the hand, the elbow under the chin, the knee jacked up lightly into the crotch. To the bystander it looks like the man is merely being searched. In case of a serious kickback, a bystander can usually be found who will testify that the suspect was only being searched and suddenly he tried to strike one of the arresting officers.

When the customer being jostled loses his head and fights back, Gilman and De Rider really go to work.

I kept the lid on. Buttons snapped off my shirt and the sun glasses shattered on the street. I turned away from the expected kick. A crowd had gathered. I fell back against my car and grinned at them. Gilman looked at me with contempt. De Rider spat on my fender.

"Did I park overtime?" I asked Powy.

"Let me really cream that bastard," Gilman grunted.

"Both of you get in the car," Powy said lazily. "Cliff'll ride me back over town."

He sat beside me. His big belly rested comfortably on his thighs. I started up and drove out as soon as the prowl car was out of the way.

"The boys don't like you much, Cliff," he said regretfully.

"That's a shame."

"If I have to pull you in, they're going to give you a hard time. You rode 'em too hard when you were on top."

"They were better cops then than they are now, Chief."

"They didn't have as much fun. But they still got a lot of spirit. Yes, sir, it's good to see the spirit of those men. They're going to leave no stone unturned to revenge that poor woman and get them jewels back. The whole city's behind us, Cliff. Yes, sir, the whole city. Any man damn fool enough to even be suspected of having dealings with them murderers is going to be spittin' teeth from now on in."

"So?"

"We shut our eyes when that insurance company you work for made deals around here in the past. But this time we ain't goin' to play that way. This is a brutal murder, son. We got our lines out in places you wouldn't even think of. I happen to know that a right big piece of money come into the local account of the insurance company in the Florence City Bank first thing this morning. And within a half hour from the time it's drawed out, son, you're going to be a guest of the city. Can I make it any clearer?"

"That's real bright, Chief. Freeze out any chance of a payoff here and they'll leave town and market the stuff someplace else."

I could tell by the way he bit down on his kitchen match that he hadn't thought of it that way.

"Maybe," I said, "if you were a smart cop, you'd let me make the deal, if, as, and when I get in contact, and then work on me to cross them up."

He gave a meaningless grunt.

"Go talk it over with the Commissioner. Doesn't he tell you when it's time to spit?"

"I'm right tired of you, Cliff."

"Is that right?"

"I've been thinking on it a long time. When this thing is over you're getting out of town."

"Am I?"

"You'll be God's own fool if you don't. Every time you take a drink I'll have you thrown in the tank. Every time you get in that car of yours, you'll get a traffic ticket. You'll learn about ordinances you never even dreamed of."

I pulled up in front of headquarters. "Go in and phone the Commissioner, Chief. Give him my love. Tell him for me that you're a fat, pompous old fud dangling next to him on the end of Tony Lavery's string."

He grunted his way out of the car, easing his belly tenderly through the door. He looked at me and shook his head sadly. "You could have been in line for my job, Bartells. You could have had just about anything you wanted in this town. But you have to go and get religion about some stinkin' bum of a wild kid. It sure is a damn shame." He duck-walked away, leaning over backward to counterbalance the weight of the big belly, clucking and shaking his head sadly.

4

At six-fifteen and a half I drove down Derecha Street through the blue-purple dusk. When I was fifty feet from the Coral Strand I saw Melody standing waiting at the curb, slim and tall. It is hard to know what to expect. I had anticipated a long wait. It was a good guess that she was out there on time because she guessed that I had expected to be kept waiting.

Dusk took the gold out her hair and left it shining silver. I pulled up beside her, reached over, and swung the door open for her. She stooped and looked in at me before climbing in. She put a folded red cape on the seat between us. She wore no hat. Her dress was severe and white with three large red buttons to keep it from looking like a uniform.

"I had to be sure it was you. Some wolves, junior grade, have been cruising by."

"Thus showing their good taste."

"Now you're starting off on the wrong foot, Mr. Bartells. I don't want to hear anything that sounds remotely personal or complimentary."

"At your service, Miss Chance." I rolled the wagon north along Derecha and turned east on Howland Road.

"Where are we going?" she asked.

"Tampa. A good place to eat. It's about a two-hour

drive and I have a hunch that any talk we might try to have in this town would be interrupted."

She settled back in the seat. Two blocks along How-land Road I noticed the car without lights dawdling along behind us. I took a right, a left, another left, and a right back out onto Howland Road.

"This sounds pretty trite, Miss Chance, but we *are* being followed."

"What do you plan to do about it?"

"Run away from them."

"In this?"

"She might surprise you."

"O.K. So I'm waiting."

As soon as I crossed the city limits I put the gas pedal down to the floor. My car has a shortened stroke, a high-compression head, and dual carburetors with control knobs on the dash. The shortened stroke makes her logy at speeds below fifty. As soon as the needle was up to seventy the stranger behind us put on his lights and began to eat up the distance between us.

"Here we go," I said above the rush of the wind, and reached out to change the carburetors to the right spot.

At eighty she began to whine nicely. The needle moved quickly around, bounced off the hundred post a few times, and then pasted itself there while the car continued to increase speed. I carry two big sacks of beach sand in the back end. The frame is reinforced.

The road stretched clear ahead. I managed to glance quickly at Melody. She had moved forward onto the edge of the seat. Her lips were slightly parted, her eyes almost closed. The lights faded 'way back. I held it at max for a good ten minutes, then dropped it back to eighty. As I did so, Melody came out of her trance and leaned back in the seat.

"How fast was that?" she asked. Her voice shook.

"Around one-twenty, I think."

She reached out and patted the dashboard. "I take back that snide remark, car."

"It forgives you, Melody. How did you feel when I had it on the top?"

"Odd. Very odd. Like I couldn't move or speak or breathe, even."

I smiled to myself and thought of other girls who had sat on my right when the crate moved up into the high numbers. Kathy, screaming against the wind, half fright and half exhilaration. And I remembered one in particular, a pale-eyed redhead I had taken home to Miami. The very extent of her steel control had intrigued me, and I had made a pass that I hadn't planned on making. She had suffered the kiss in thin, tight-lipped silence and then said, "This is a little silly, isn't it?"

Out of anger I had punched the crate up to a speed where the wind screamed like a thousand devils. The redhead took that top speed in grim silence for ten thundering miles before something within her snapped and she moved over against me on the seat, her head loose on the slender throat. When I stopped the car the second time her mouth had been like a soft open wound.

All of them are alike. They're like the locks I used to buy in the dime store when I was a kid, with rings that you set so that it made a certain combination of numbers. But with the females, the rings contain letters rather than numbers, and you have to be smart enough to set them so that the letters spell out a word. For the redhead the word had been danger. With Kathy the mystic combination was the word marriage.

Now I looked over at Melody's clear profile against the night and I wondered what the combination would be for her. I wondered whether, if I found it, I would want to use it. It would not be an emotional attachment. I wanted no part of any emotional attachment. It would be a game, like working on one of those locks until you hit the right number. And that was all it would be. I had a funny kind of weariness in me. The odd part was sensing that Melody had it too.

I felt her eyes on me. "So you're not married, Mr. Bartells."

"How do you figure?"

"A wife would make you give up this toy of yours. Most of them would."

"Are you an expert on how wives react?"

"I was one myself, once upon a time. You see, I keep his name. Chance. More rhythmic, don't you think, than Melody Stegman? I use the Miss to keep from compounding the confusion."

"Did it suit you? Marriage?"

"What's your name again? Cliff? Put it this way. It suited what I was. I don't know if it would suit me now.

What do they say? It takes seven years for every part of you to change. I guess we're like lizards, shedding a thousand skins a year. When I was twenty I was a gay little bride. Now, Cliff, I'm twenty-seven, and I'm not so very gay."

"When I was one and twenty . . ." I said softly.

"Tell me about you at one and twenty, Cliff. Don't you get the feeling that they're still back there, in the past, the people we were once upon a time, still laughing and loving and not knowing what will happen?"

"Now we go mystic, eh? There was nothing mystic about me at twenty-one. I was a he-maid in a tourist court in Florence City. I bet I changed forty beds a day. You learn a lot about humanity, changing their linen, you know. The boss had a daughter. I suppose if I could hop in my time machine and go back there and take a look at her, I would have her cased. I would see the round heels. But to me, back there, she was the angel of all angels. Her name was, and is, Connie. My true beloved. On the hottest days the body scent of her would come through the perfume and the deodorant, very delicately tart. It made me dizzy, that scent. We had a storeroom. One side of it was piled high with mattresses and pillows. It had no windows, and it was like a furnace in there in the summer. I guess her people had us figured out, all right. Now I know why the old man didn't raise hell. I guess he figured that I was keeping Connie at home, at least. And besides, I was going to be a cop and we were going to live happily ever after, especially after I got my pension and we could watch our grandchildren grow up. I talk too much, don't I? I got to be a cop and later I went into the Army. I see Connie on the street sometimes. She always smiles."

"You surprise me, Cliff."

"What did you expect?"

"We *are* being frank, aren't we? No fencing. You annoyed me on the beach. You realize that, of course. I decided right away about you. I decided you are a type I don't care much for. One of those men who always plots himself as the hero of a very bitter James M. Cain novel. The muscular, side-of-the-mouth, 'Come here, baby' sort. The man who thinks that because he has all the usual muscles and most of his hair, he's irresistible to all females. Now you have me wondering."

"Why?"

"Men like that always make themselves the hero of their little stories. In the Connie story you don't come out so well. That's what surprises me. Of course, I do detect a certain amount of bitterness. Why did you stop being a cop, Cliff?"

"The opportunities for advancement are too limited."

"Now I've asked the wrong question, haven't I? Your voice is different."

"Who's your ex-husband married to now?"

"Not that color widow, Cliff. I'm the legitimate kind. Dave Chance was a very sweet guy. Not too awfully bright, I guess, but I thought so at the time. No money and no social position, much to Aunt Elizabeth's horror. A war marriage, of course. He was a naval aviator, and they had him instructing at Pensacola. We lived in a room there. You know—borrowed-time stuff. A little chintzy room. I was storing up all the memories, locking them away fast like packing trunks, against the day when he'd go overseas. Then one afternoon Commander Moore, his boss, came in a staff car and held both my hands very tight and said that a bos'n's mate named Dockerty had run over Dave in a Navy jeep and killed him. I was bracing myself for high tragedy at some time in the future. The Navy Department wire and all that, with Dave dead three thousand miles away. But there he was, dead in Pensacola. Just like the parachute jumper who falls off the back steps. Poor Commander Moore. I took a deep breath and roared, just roared with laughter. Of course, it turned into hysterics and they gave me shots and all that, but that first laugh is probably something the Commander will never forget."

"What did you do then?"

"I went back to Boston and took a grim little room in Chelsea and worked in a bookstore near the Common."

She didn't elaborate, and the lights of Tampa were in the distance before either of us broke the silence again.

"You're very special, Melody," I said finally. "In a funny way."

"I'm not special, Cliff. I'm too tired of—of things to be special. Tired of fighting and tired of trying and tired of believing in things. Sooner or later I'm always told I'm special, as though it's the highest possible compliment."

"I didn't mean it as a compliment and I wasn't talking

about the visible aspects of the problem. It's no news to you, Melody, that your face is neither pretty nor beautiful, but very striking, which is maybe better than to have it any other way, and you're put together by somebody who enjoyed his work and did well by you. So to hell with this compliment angle."

"Are you trying to be rough, Cliff?"

"Not rough. Objective. You're special because most women with your visible advantages spend all their time grabbing or posing, and I haven't seen you do either yet. You talk my language and I don't know how to go about making you, and I may even give up the whole idea."

I had spoken with more heat than I had expected to show. She said gently, "It would be a very good idea to give up, Cliff."

By this time we were entering Tampa, and I jockeyed the car through the traffic in the direction of Ybor City. Melody wondered about it and I told her. The city fathers have, for some time, had the rather vague idea of turning Ybor City into something resembling the French Quarter in New Orleans. But there isn't enough to start with. Ybor City is what you would get if you took the flavor and atmosphere of one square block of old New Orleans and scattered it, diluted it over thirty or forty blocks of depressed ex-residential, semi-industrial area in any U.S. city. A lot of the best food is served in tile palaces that look like annexes to the men's room in Grand Central, and you can get the same food next to a patio fountain with colored lights shining on it—if you want to pay the differential.

Ybor City was alive and awake after a long dull day, and laughter was harsh on the street corners. Melody sat in her corner with a certain wariness. I parked and she stood waiting while I locked the car, and we walked together to Mamma Fernandez' place.

"It's a good place," I said as I pushed open the door. Pritch, from the *Tampa Times*, was standing at the bar. He gave me a cool nod. Pepe, Mamma's eldest, was tending bar. Off to the right of the bar were wire-legged tables and chairs, none of them set for service. Mamma came bustling in from the kitchen, wiping her hands on her apron. I had called her earlier; she was expecting us.

Since Mamma looks like the movie version of the hefty Mexican matriarch, it is a considerable surprise to hear her talk with the flat nasal tones of Indiana, where she was born and raised.

"My God, Cliff, you're getting sense, going out with a tall girl. Come, darlings, I'm putting you in the smallest room, and don't look like that, girl. This is purely a restaurant I'm running. What's your name. Chance? Right back here, come along."

As Melody followed her through the curtains, I glanced back over my shoulder. Pritch had a speculative look on his face. I could almost hear the wheels turning. It was bad luck that he had to be there, but it couldn't be helped.

The smallest room is surprising. The walls are paneled in cypress and there is a tiny fireplace for the few cool months of the year. The tablecloth was chalk-white under the light of the two candles. The room is not larger than ten by ten.

I slid Melody's chair in and went around and sat down, facing her. She smiled. "It's nice here!"

"The best is yet to come, Melody."

First came the tiny shrimp, cooked in garlic and oil, with Mamma advising us to dawdle over them and over the manzanilla wine so that the main course could be prepared.

We ate like a pair of wolves. The wine flushed our faces, and looking across at her, I found I had made an error in telling her that she was not beautiful. Then Mamma proudly brought in the hot casserole of *paella*. Melody had never eaten it before. *Paella* is an adventure, particularly when it is lovingly prepared by Mamma Fernandez. Melody made warm small sounds in her throat as she came upon the clams in their open shells, the white breasts of chicken, the half-inch cubes of tenderloin. She was wary of the octopus, but willing to try it, and then sorry there wasn't more of it.

When it was all gone Mamma brought in the pot of coffee, her special coffee, so strong that you can almost stand the spoon in it.

There was a comfortable and friendly silence. One of Mamma's meals is an experience shared.

"What came before Pensacola?" I asked. "I've got to sort you out."

"Sorting me out, I suppose, depends on understanding Aunt Elizabeth. My father was her younger brother. To drop into the vernacular, before the depression, when I was quite small, we were loaded. Dad was a partner in a Boston brokerage house. We had a place on the Cape. I got a horse for my birthday when I was six. That was in 1929. Dad had a sixty-foot boat. We had three cars. I guess I was a pretty snotty little brat. Private schools and all that. An only child. Spoiled through and through. Of course, I didn't know what was going on. Dad's lawyer told me years later, the year I got out of school. Both Dad and Aunt Elizabeth were in the market. Very heavily. She got scared in the summer of 1929 and got out. As the older sister, she insisted that Dad get out too. He laughed at her. Nothing could go wrong with the world. Aunt Elizabeth was not a woman you could cross.

"Those were the happy years, I guess. They're pretty dim in my mind. Aunt Elizabeth converted all of her holdings—most of them, anyway—into government bonds. In 1930 Dad went to her and pleaded with her to bail him out. They were about to sell him out because he couldn't put up the margin. She told him that she had warned him.

"A week later Dad killed himself. He used the typical brokerage procedure in those days. He went out a high window. Mother died eight months later. They left me two things: a little money—enough to get me through school in Switzerland—and a lot of hate. I think it was hate of Aunt Elizabeth that killed Mother. It poisoned her. And she told me never to have anything to do with her. Things like that make a terrible impression on kids. I couldn't understand why, but I knew that Aunt Elizabeth was, in some way, responsible for what had happened.

"The hate lasted longer than the money did. I suppose any person less determined than Aunt Elizabeth would have given up. She didn't. She tried to run my life. I was the only close relative left. She couldn't admit defeat. I sent back countless gifts—beautiful, expensive gifts. She was at her worst when I was twenty, trying to block my marriage to Dave Chance. You see, she didn't have any hold over me because I had never taken a dime from her. But she kept on trying.

"It's really funny, in a way, that Dave was the one who gave me the first doubts. I told him the whole story once. He said that Aunt Elizabeth was right, that no amount of money she could have given Dad would have saved him. He was in too deeply and the stocks dropped too far. Aunt Elizabeth's money would have gone down the same hole his did, and then there would have been no money at all in the family. He told me I shouldn't be so rough on the old girl. I guess Dave just didn't have the capacity for hate. Well, I told you how he died. I went back to Boston, but habit is a very strong thing. I still couldn't bring myself to make peace with Aunt Elizabeth. I didn't want any close relative. I wanted to be alone, to mend alone. You know how that is.

"Well, a year ago, I called on Aunt Elizabeth. I still wouldn't let her give me anything, but I told her that I was willing to be her friend. She cried. She went all to pieces. Here was something she had tried to achieve for twenty years, and now she had it. She was a woman without real warmth, I guess. Pretty austere. But with a strong, strong sense of family. And I guess she was afraid of dying alone. Maybe she regretted never marrying. I don't know. At any rate, I used to go and have tea with her once a week, on Sunday afternoons. The third time or the fourth, I forget, a man named Furness Trumbull was there.

"I hadn't seen Furny since I was a little kid. His people had a summer place near ours. He was about fourteen when I was six, and I remembered him because he used to take me out in his little catboat. His people lost their money at the same time Dad lost his. Furny had never made any of it back, but Trumbull is a good name in Boston. There isn't much to Furny, I guess. He makes himself agreeable to wealthy old ladies. He's always a house guest somewhere.

"It wasn't enough for Aunt Elizabeth to get me back into the fold. She wanted to marry me off to Trumbull. I guess maybe she wanted to see children in the family again before she died. Furny, of course, knew that to marry me would open Aunt Elizabeth's purse strings for him. But I'll give the man a little credit and say he was and is genuinely attracted to me. Between the two of them they began to put on the pressure. By then, seven or eight months ago, I was the manager of the bookstore. I quit and went down to New York City with my savings. A model agency took me on. Then a funny thing happened. I began to get lonely for Aunt Elizabeth. I began to feel sorry for her. Furny came down, week end after week end, to talk me into going back to Boston. I didn't want to go. Then, in December, Aunt Elizabeth and Furny came down in her car and Aunt Elizabeth pleaded with me. She told me that Furny loved me, and that he had become almost a son to her. Furny sat there and beamed at me. He asked me to marry him.

"They kept at me until finally we reached a compromise. Aunt Elizabeth said she was coming down here to Florida and that Furny would come down too. She wanted to pay my way and have me come down also, with the idea that the three of us would be in a new environment and maybe I would see things in a different light.

"Cliff, there comes a time when you get tired of fighting. I agreed to come along, and I suppose I was acknowledging defeat right there, because I expected, without admitting it to myself, that I would let Furny talk me into marriage. A woman gets tired of that kind of life where there's no razor on the bathroom shelf, no pipe on the mantel. They both kept at me until I agreed to come down here. The Franklins drove Aunt Elizabeth down and she got to Florence City early in January. Furny couldn't come with her. He wanted to come down with me in my little car, but I said no, and he flew down, using money that I guess Aunt Elizabeth gave him, and got here a few days after I arrived. The three of us have been going places together, with Aunt Elizabeth paying the bills. Furny is staying over at the Baybright, two blocks below Aunt Elizabeth's apartment.

"Well, we've had some scenes. Oh, very polite scenes with everybody speaking in soft voices, but scenes just the same. I let Furny kiss me and there was nothing there. I couldn't bring myself to say yes to him. It made Furny pretty moody. The idea was that if I would agree to marry him, Aunt Elizabeth would stake us to a round-the-world cruise lasting a full year, and she would come along too. I know that sounds a little ridiculous. And she kept telling me that she was leaving me everything in her will. Aunt Elizabeth was not the sort of woman who can see anyone's point of view but her own. She kept at me because of the horrid little place where I'm living. I gave in on one point. The day before she was killed, I agreed to move into the Tide Winds with her as soon as the week was up. I suppose, if nothing had happened, I would just have made one concession after another until I found myself bedded with Furny."

"And now?"

She looked at me with a somber expression. "I might still marry him. He's being insistent. He keeps telling me that it's what Aunt Elizabeth would have wanted. He knows that I'm going to get all the money now. I keep thinking that it's the money that my father wanted, that she wouldn't let him have. It isn't good money to have, Cliff."

"Money has no memory."

"Now you have me sorted out. Now you know everything about me worth knowing, Cliff. Now you can tell me what you meant when you said something about trusting me this afternoon on the beach. I know you're with the insurance company."

I drew marks with my thumbnail on the tablecloth. I told her the story. I told her where I fitted. I told her that I was willing to pay $325,000 for the return of the stones, no questions asked. I told her that she had already answered the main question I wanted to ask: Who would profit from her aunt's death through association with Melody? The answer, of course, was Furness Trumbull.

After going through it, I looked up at her. She was staring at me.

"I don't understand what you're doing, Cliff. The way you explain it, you're going to lose either way by working on this case. It doesn't sound very bright."

I stared hard at her. "And how about you? What did you have to gain by coming down here?"

"That's different. I'd just got to the point where nothing seemed very important any more."

"And you're the only one in the world that could happen to, I suppose."

"You use sarcasm like a club, Mr. Bartells."

"Part of never growing up is the conviction that you're unique, baby."

"If you think Furny could kill an old lady, you're more naïve than unique."

We glared hard at each other. But unlike that m[...] on the beach, no grins arrived to dissolve it[...] paid Mamma, she sensed the mood immedia[...] me a pitying look. I helped Melody [...]

around her shoulders. I shut her into the car, got behind the wheel, and headed back through the city to our route.

I tried to reason out my anger with her. When I was painfully honest in my analysis, I found that her indecision as to whether or not to marry Furny now that the aunt was dead had started my annoyance. And that was ridiculous. I didn't care who she married or how often. A man is either a man or a boy. But a woman can be a twist, a broad, a bim, a skirt, a dish, a piece, or half a hundred other names, many of them savage, most of them earthy. It is interesting from a philological point of view. I drove staring straight ahead down the shafts of light, and I told myself that this was another one. Just pick the right word. Push the right buttons. Turn to the right combination.

Three miles from Florence City, I wrenched the car off onto the sandy shoulder, fighting it and slowing it down as it bounced and slewed.

I cut the lights and motor and reached for her. "Just what was expected," she said acidly in the darkness.

I slipped my hand under the cape and down to the concave place at the small of her back and pulled her roughly to me, finding her unresisting lips in the darkness. The spice of the food was still heavy on her breath. She came limp and lax into my arms, like a sand-stuffed dummy, and, feeling a perfect fool, I continued the kiss on and on, getting nothing from it or from her.

I let her go. "Enjoy it?" she asked. She laughed.

I growled something at her. I started the motor and turned on the lights. "Wait a minute, Cliff," she said. I turned toward her. She was smiling. She came over against me and wound both fists up in the lapels of my jacket and kissed me on the lips. The kiss burned like candle wax that drips on the back of your hand. Fire came out of her and seared the night.

As I reached for her she pushed herself violently away. "N—— me home, Cliff. Quickly, please."

—— in front of the Coral Strand. "I'm sorry,

——hink I know what it is, in you. Sort of a ——even, isn't it? Never mind. Please don't ——. She slipped out quickly and pushed ——ched her walk under the night light

5

Harry Banson came into the diner the next morning when I was halfway through breakfast. He got coffee at the counter and came over to the booth.

"Good morning. Aren't you being pretty brave, Harry? Lots of people might see you sitting with me."

"Lay off," he said sullenly. He lifted a spoonful of coffee and blew on it before putting it in his mouth. The spoon rattled off his yellow teeth.

"Officially," he said, "I'm warning you. Powy told me to hunt you up."

"He get stuck in his swivel chair?"

"Damn you, Cliff, I'm doing the best I can. He told me to hunt you up and give you the word."

"Keep talking."

"He says any more reckless driving inside the city limits and you get your license lifted."

I leaned back. It answered a few questions. "Who was in the prowl car? Gilman and De Rider? You take this back to Powy. You tell him I was well under the speed limit until I crossed the city line. From there on, what I do is none of his business."

Harry Banson wiped his mouth on the back of his hand. The moisture flattened out the curly black hair on the back of his hand. I watched it spring up, hair by hair, as he rested his yellowish hand in the sunlight on the table.

"So I told you. Now maybe I can ask you why you pull a damn fool thing like taking that Chance girl out of town."

"Sure you can ask me. Ask me again."

He sighed. "I'm asking you again."

"Because, as representative of the Security Theft and Accident Insurance Company, Incorporated, I find it necessary to contact the policy holder. Since the policy holder happens to be dead, I am forced to contact the next person in line, the person who will receive either the stolen gems or the face value of the policy."

"Powy doesn't want you in this one."

"Then I suggest he contact my employers and tell them about it. I work for a living."

"You just got no sense, Cliff. No sense at all."

He went to the cash register and paid his dime check and went out, squinting against the sunlight, his shirt stuck to his back. The unseasonable February heat was continuing, and it had an odd stickiness about it more typical of August than of February.

I walked down to the office, gave sallow Wilma Booton a broad wink, and went into my office. Mart was out on a couple of routine investigations. Arthur Myers was out too. Kathy came into my office and shut the door behind her.

"Gosh, Cliff. It's exciting, isn't it?"

I stared hard at the neckline dip of her dress. "It certainly is."

"You stop that. Are you going to make a recovery on the stones, Cliff?"

I spoke out of the corner of my mouth. "We can't talk here, kid. Come on over to my place about eight tonight."

She threw her shoulders back. "You know very darn well I'm never going up to that apartment of yours, and besides, I have a date with Andy tonight."

"Ah. Andrew Hope Maybree the Third. Keep away from those teeth, sugar. You could get a bad laceration."

"Andy's a very serious type." This was said with great contempt for all the Cliffs of this world.

"Ask him to tell you the one about the three old ladies on the train."

Her eyes went wide and then, under her deep tan, a flush crept up from her throat. It was a dead giveaway. She yanked the door open and fled, my laughter following her.

I walked back and got in the car and drove out to the Baybright. A haughty young lady with pinch-on glasses stared over my head and asked me if I were a friend of Mr. Trumbull. I explained that I was, in a manner of speaking. She unbent a little bit and told me that Mr. Trumbull was "taking" breakfast on the terrace overlooking the pool. He would be outside Apartment K.

He would be, and he was. He sat at a small table in the sun, wearing swimming trunks with a green porpoise embroidered on the right pants leg. He was reading a folded paper that looked to be the air edition of the *New York Times*.

He glanced up at me with that absent look reserved for the help. "Well?"

I pulled a chair away from the row against the wall and put it near the table where it would still be in the shade.

"Have I had the pleasure?" he asked, in the tone of voice that indicated that there could never be any pleasure in it.

"Melody told me to look you up, Mr. Trumbull."

He was quick on his feet. "Ah! How nice! You're a friend of hers, of course."

"One of the best. Lovely girl, Melody."

We stared at each other. I wanted him to ask me what I wanted. He was equally determined to let me fumble it out by myself. The guy was built. No question of it. Heavy shoulders and good clean arm muscles. He had that baked-in tan that never completely disappears. Crisp brown hair and brown eyes. He had that look of fading and superficial boyishness which seems to appeal to the dowager set. I knew the type from seeing a lot of them in postwar Florence City. Having no money themselves, they have managed, through a sharpening of the instinct for survival, to fasten themselves to the moneyed groups.

The tweedy, stag-line, Cannes, horsy, column-bait, so charming chiselers. The rich collect them like kings of old collected court jesters. And these boys know when to play the clown, when to apply the bite, which bedrooms to stay out of, and which ones to frequent. Amateur touts at the races, sharpies at the bridge table, heavy winners at canasta, they manage to live the parasite's existence with considerable studied charm.

They set off the parties, rhumba like experts, bully the waiters. And, when their luck is in, they marry a Melody Chance and live at last in the way they have been pretending to live all along.

"Melody tells me, Mr. Trumbull, that before her aunt's tragic death, there was some talk of you two being married."

The sun heat made the sweat run down through the triangular patch of hair on his broad chest. He laughed in great delight. "That *is* amusing, Mr. . . ."

"Bartells. Cliff Bartells."

"Forgive me for laughing, Mr. Bartells, but it struck me funny. It's in poor taste to laugh at such a time, I know. I'm afraid Melody was a little reticent with you if she said anything about 'some talk' of our being married. My dear fellow, there's no question of it. Of course, this has been a horrid shock to Melody. There's so much to do, with the lawyers arriving and all, and the body to be sent to Boston for burial. We are having to put marriage out of our minds for the time being, but once it is all over, that poor child and I will be married and go away together. Someone has got to help her get over this. She was desperately fond of Miss Stegman, you know."

I took his cigarettes off the table and lit one. I puffed the smoke toward him. "She kept this great love under a barrel, I guess."

"I've known Melody since she was a small child. Who are you, anyway?"

I grinned at him. "I'm the guy who's trying to contact the thieves and buy back the junk jewelry for three hundred and seventy-five thousand bucks, Trumbull."

The only sign of anger was the knotting of his jaw muscles. "In other words, you lied to me, Bartells. You're no friend of Melody's."

"You can't be sure, though, can you?"

He gave me a wide boyish smile, but the brown eyes were cool. "If you really don't mind, old boy, I would like to read the paper."

I stood up. "Nice for you the old lady is dead, with you marrying the heiress and all."

I couldn't rock him. He didn't lose his smile. "I suppose you feel you have to say things like that, being sort of a semipoliceman or something. It must make you feel more like a man, probably. Permit me to think in your terms, old boy. Regardless of whether she lived or died, I was in a position to profit, you might say."

"How about if Melody doesn't marry you?"

"That's my personal affair, and the idea is absurd anyway. You might check with your local police. You'll find I'm working very closely with them. You'll also find that they are quite well convinced that I shall hound them until the murderer is found. Miss Stegman was too close to me for me to be rational about this."

Though I instinctively disliked him, I had to admire his touch. He handled me so neatly that I began to wonder if Melody had been entirely on the level with me.

"Good day, old man," he said.

I nodded gloomily at him and went back off the terrace. Some teen-agers were sloshing around in the pool, screaming at each other. I wished I could drop off too many years, leap in, and rassle the girls myself. I wished I could punch Trumbull in his patrician nose. I wished Kathy would come to the apartment. And I wished something would break, somebody would want to get in touch.

I went back to my room and climbed the open staircase. The edge of a piece of paper peeped out from under my door. I picked it up and recognized Kathy's familiar backhand.

"A call came and I suppose you'll know what it means. I don't. A man said to tell you he's got a good dog in the seventh. Have you been betting, Cliff? You told me that was for sucker tourists. Kathy."

I walked in, leaving the door open, and cursed Kathy for being an empty-headed fool. All cops aren't dense. Powy might have made sense out of that note, given enough time. I was sorry that I'd told Johnny Alfrayda that Kathy could be trusted. She was completely trustworthy in one sense, of course. But this sort of lapse could be dangerous.

I stripped off my shirt and put the phone base on my chest as I dialed the office from the comfort of the day bed. I got hold of Kathy.

"Don't say anything but short answers, darlin'. How long ago did that call come in?"

"About ten minutes after you left the office. You sound mad, Cliff."

"I am. Shut up. Now get this straight. If the same joker calls again, you tell him this: 'Cliff has his bet down.' "

"Cliff has his bet down," she repeated in a small obedient voice. She sounded so crushed that I relented.

"You're a good girl, Kathy. I'm not mad any more. Tonight you ask Andy to tell you the one about the talking dog in the barroom."

She gasped and hung up. I lay there, grinning like a fool.

At four o'clock I was in Tampa. Any man who knew the tracks well might have made the connection between the message and Johnny Alfrayda. I left the car in a downtown garage and walked four blocks before catching a taxi out to his house. I had the cabby let me off three blocks from Johnny's place.

Johnny had a rough time as a kid. When the dough began to come in, and it came in fast and in large coarse amounts, he built the kind of house he had always wanted. It would make an architect scream and froth at the mouth. It is bastard Gothic, Spanish, and château, with a dash of Georgian. Out in the back gardens is a whole batch of concrete mushrooms eight feet high, with bronze frogs as big as St. Bernards under them. The wall around the place is twelve feet high and it has broken glass set in the top.

Johnny went into semiretirement when the syndicate took over his areas. He decided that he couldn't work for them, wouldn't work with them, and was too small-time to fight them. It was a smart decision.

Johnny looks like the movie version of a big dumb gorilla. Arms like tree limbs and little bandy legs and, eyes set deep under shelves of bone. Blue jowls and one mashed ear.

The ever faithful Oscar let me in the front gate and told me that Johnny was out in back with the kids. There are about ten kids, half his and half adopted. Johnny grinned at me and chased them all away. We went and sat on a park bench he had taken from some city of temporary residence and stared at his flower beds.

He pounded my shoulder, nearly knocking me off the bench. "How come it's got to be business before I see you?"

"I know. I know. My fault."

Johnny's only occupation is that of middleman. I had met him on a previous recovery case. It had gone as smooth as nylon.

"Cliff, I been watching this thing. I been hoping it wouldn't come knocking on my door. This is a bad one, Cliff. This one smells."

"I've been hearing that every five minutes for nearly three days. It's not news."

"I check, Cliff, and I find you in on it and I get surprised. You know what I mean. I say to myself the Cliff's got more sense. Maybe he's tired of the work, huh?"

"Just tired."

"Those punk cops you got down there, Cliff! Terrible. I know a deal like this. The same like I would have handled it in the old days if anything like that goes on in my back yard. Bad for business. Bad for everybody's business. I would have stuck needles in every cop in town until it got cleaned up. And if any insurance guy started a dicker to get the stuff back, I'd have the cops work on him until he'd agree to cross up the boys who did the job."

"You haven't said anything new yet, Johnny."

He sighed. "O.K., O.K. Now comes the new stuff. I got the call this morning. From a pay booth, I guess. A guy, talking low. Says I was recommended to him but he won't say by who. Tells me to get in touch with the insurance guy and get set for the pay-off. Says he's got the stones. Told me he'd call again and then he hung up. Just before he hung up, like an afterthought, he gave me the price."

"And?"

"Four hundred thousand, Cliff. Everything goes through right, I get my five per cent. Twenty thousand. Not exactly hay, Cliff. But somehow I don't like the smell of it. The guy is talking probably through a handkerchief, but I can smell how nervous he is. He won't give me any more information. Not a scrap. I think and think and then decided to talk to you about it. You want my opinion, I say keep your head up. It all smells bad."

"How bad?"

"Take it this way. One murder. Everybody after them. Nothing to lose. So get the four hundred grand and keep the stones too. They'll expect a cross, so they'll cross you first. My advice, stay away from it. Resign. Move up here. I'll get you a job. Anything you like."

"No, thanks. I'm in it now. I'm staying in it."

"I don't want to help you, Cliff. Twenty thousand says go ahead. Something else says no. Good sense, maybe."

"Go ahead with it, Johnny. I'll keep my guard up. If they don't go through you, they'll go through somebody else. And I'd rather it was you."

He slapped his big hands down onto thick thighs. "O.K. What do I tell him when he calls me up again?"

"Tell them it will take a little time to get the money lined up. Tell them if they'll be patient, we'll play ball. Stall them a little."

He stared at me. "Stall them, huh? What you got on your mind, Cliff?"

"A bonus from the company. I'll be in touch."

As I walked around the corner of the house I looked back and saw him sitting there, massive and inert, as seemingly lifeless as the concrete mushrooms, the bronze frogs. The kids, seeing me leave, were hollering down toward him, leaping the flower beds.

I drove slowly back to Florence City. I ate after dusk in a drive-in on the outskirts of town. There were two ways to figure it, and I didn't know which way I liked. Either the figure of four hundred thousand had come out of the thin air, or it had come from the hood-eyed Horace Franklin. My little gag had been to tell everybody a different amount and then listen for the echo to come back. I decided that I had been a dope to give out such round figures.

The shoe didn't fit the Franklins perfectly because of the eagerness with which Letty Franklin had lunged at the idea of making a few extra bucks. It didn't seem logical that, with potential big dough in the immediate future, she'd foul up the act by reaching for something much smaller. I could still hear the meaty sound of her husband's hand as he had struck her. His actions, at the time, had seemed a little extreme. In the light of what had happened, his actions began to make sense . . . only if he were in on it and Letty was left in the dark.

There was diagonal parking in front of the beer joint known as the Bomb Run. I pulled into an open slot and walked in. The bar was on the right. Two pin-ball machines and a juke box were against the back wall. The table shuffleboard—shovelboard to the initiate—ran along the left wall, one of the new eleven-hundred-dollar models with electric scoring and coin slots. A few hamburgs were spattering on the grill at the end of the bar and they gave off an odor that was not exactly triple-A beef. The overhead lighting was garish, big fluorescent fixtures that threw a hard and unflattering glare down onto the tables.

I sat on a bar stool and took inventory. All but two tables were taken. The Franklins weren't around. A blackboard hung near the shuffleboard with the names of the challengers written on it. Two couples were playing each other, the women at one end, the men at the other. One of the women was an expert, shooting the weights with either hand. The women maintained a competitive silence. The men kidded each other.

Midway through the second bottle of beer, as I was considering leaving, the Franklins came in, Horace first, Letty following. They went over to one of the two empty tables. Horace walked back and wrote "H & L" on the challenge board. Letty bobbed her head at acquaintances. The proprietor went out from behind the bar and took their beer orders. Letty's eyes swept across me, stopped, and came warily back. She decided to smile and then changed her mind. She leaned toward Horace and whispered to him.

He looked directly at me. The overhead lights made blue-green glints on his slicked-down hair. He didn't change expression as I picked up my bottle and my glass and started toward their table.

6

I GAVE THE TWO of them my best off-duty smile as I neared their table. Letty smiled a bit timidly, but Horace continued the stony stare.

"Hope you don't mind," I said, putting my bottle and glass on the table.

"Not at all," Horace said. "Sit down."

"I can't remember whether I told you my name. I'm Cliff Bartells."

"The insurance man," Horace said.

"Don't remind me. I'm not working at it tonight. I want to forget the whole deal. Every once in a while a stinker like this comes along." I drummed up a gleam in the eye and looked over at Letty. "The only break I get is when there are blondes mixed up in it."

"Oh, you!" she said, doing a little writhe in her chair. She was a chunk. Evidently that pale blue sun suit of hers had a skirt that could be worn in place of the shorts. I was sure it was the same halter top. As she moved there was a strong flex of muscles across the bare midriff.

Horace allowed himself a sour smile that pinched up one corner of his mouth. Letty's nose bothered me. It was as thin as the blade of a knife and the tip of it was pink and pendulous. I lifted my glass to drink, and I blotted out the nose with a finger. The effect was to turn her into an amazingly handsome woman. Her eyes were particularly lovely. It made my part easier to play. The left side of her mouth was a bit puffy from Horace's love tap the previous afternoon.

"Well, you're having a sort of vacation," I said jovially.

"Fine!" Horace said. "We're dipping into our savings. The damn cops won't let us head back. I saw the Chance girl today. She gave me the cold eye and told me to be patient. The lawyer's due tomorrow. We've got to see about getting another position, Bartells."

"I'm sure Miss Chance will do the right thing," I said.

Horace sniffed and looked away. The man had brought two large steins of draught. Letty dipped thirstily into hers, tilting it higher and higher as her strong throat worked. When she set it down there was an inch left in the bottom of it and there was a dab of foam on the tip of her nose. She scooped it off with her knuckle.

"That's what I needed," she said.

I gave her my boyish smile. "You know, I always had an entirely different idea of . . . of people who work for . . ."

"Of servants?" Horace said with a snicker.

"That's right. I never expected to find an attractive couple like you in this sort of setup."

"That," said Horace, "is because you never heard about the rates. You take our job. We've worked for Miss Stegman since '46. The work isn't hard. Driving, housework, some cooking, a little lawn work, keeping the car in shape, some washing and ironing. Three hundred and fifteen dollars a month plus board and room for the pair of us." He warmed to his explanation, leaning toward me. "What does another couple without that kind of job pay for shelter? All told, maybe seventy-five. Food is maybe another eighty. So figure our total take at four-seventy a month, and we only have to pay taxes on the three-fifteen. All my cigarettes came out of what she bought to keep on hand for parties. And once in a while a bottle could disappear. The trouble is, people think there's something low about being a servant. I say let them think so. I'll take the cash on the line."

"I never realized it that way before," I said.

"And besides," he said, "you get a chance to move around. Summers on the Cape, a month or so down here every winter. A trip to New York every now and then. You can't beat it, can you?"

I signaled for another round. "I guess you can't," I said. I moved my foot cautiously under the table until it touched Letty's. Her foot moved away quickly. I left mine there, felt her foot come back hesitantly and touch mine. I gave it a gentle pressure, then looked at her. She seemed a bit flustered. She dug into her white purse for cigarettes and matches. As she was lighting her own cigarette, I put one in my mouth and said, "Hold the light."

She held the match out. I took her wrist firmly in my hand to steady it and looked into her eyes as I lit the cigarette. There were spots of high color on her cheeks. Letty was no longer in doubt as to whether a pass was being made. Now she was positive, but she didn't know what to do about it.

Horace seemed very morose. I got a third stein of beer into Letty before their turn came to play. As challengers they had to feed the four nickels to the machine. Letty played against the female of the couple who had won the previous game, and she played at the end of the board nearest where I sat. I didn't take my eyes from her and she grew extremely conscious of that fact. She tried to be graceful in every move, but her sturdy figure turned her motions into a burlesque that fell midway between comic and pathetic.

After each shot she made, she giggled. And the shots she made were terrible. Horace's glare up the length of the board grew steadily blacker. He made the only points for the partnership, and they were swamped, 21 to 11.

She came back first to the table. Horace paused at another table for a few moments, then strode to the blackboard and wrote "H & K." He was still sore when he sat down with us.

"I never saw you so lousy," he said, "not even the first night I was teaching you the game."

"Is it that important, dear?" she asked airily.

"When I play, I play to win, damnit. I'm up on the board again, but that guy named Karl Something-or-other is my partner."

"I hope you two have a lovely time, dear," she said.

For one bad moment I thought he was going to whop her right there at the table. I guessed she thought so too. She wrapped her hand around the fresh stein I had ordered for her and the muscles in her arm were very evident.

After the tension faded away, she pushed her chair back a little and crossed her heavy legs. "It's only a game, dear," she said.

He got up without a word and went through a door in the back, coyly marked "His." The one next to it, of course, was "Hers."

"It can't be much fun for you, Letty," I said, "and that makes me feel bad, because you look like a person who deserves a good time."

"What do you mean by that, Cliff?" she asked warily.

I shrugged. "I didn't mean anything. No doubt you love the guy. He just strikes me as being a pretty sour partner for a Florida vacation."

"Do you always go around criticizing a person's husband, now?"

"You talk like you think this is some kind of a line, Letty. Maybe you're forgetting something. Maybe you're forgetting that yesterday I saw him hit you when all you were doing was trying to help. It certainly made me feel awful inside to see a pretty woman slapped around like that in front of a stranger."

Her eyes went hard and she touched her fingertips to the left side of her mouth. "Someday," she said huskily, "I'm going to get even with . . . you know, this is darn good beer they serve here."

Horace came back and sat down. He gave the two of us a suspicious stare. Conversation faded and died. Letty's color was high. She kept downing the steins of beer as fast as I ordered them. Soon Horace had to leave us to play the game on the board.

"We were saying . . ." I said.

"He can be an awful louse," she said. "I admit it. I'm not hiding anything. I could tell you what a hell he's made of my life. I shouldn't talk about him like this."

"It's good for you. Get it out of your system," I said.

She gave me a grateful glance. The beer was getting to her. It took her a little space of time to adjust the focus of her eyes.

"You know, Cliff, I like you. I knew right off I was going to like you. You ever feel that way about anybody?"

"Now, there's a coincidence for you! There's a coincidence!"

She blushed like a schoolgirl and buried her confusion

in the stein of beer. She turned away and said, "Look! They won that one. Now they'll keep playing."

I leaned toward her. "You were talking about getting even with Horace, Letty. I've got an idea. The next time he goes to the men's room, let's you and me duck out of here."

"Gee, I couldn't," she said, but her eyes were bright.

"It'll do him good to worry a little. You'll be surprised how nice he'll be to you once he realizes that you're darn attractive to other men. How long since he's told you your eyes are beautiful?"

"I don't know as he ever did. Are they?"

"You know they are. I'm not thinking of anything, honestly, except just a ride in my car to cool off. Be a sport, Letty."

She gave a jerky nod. "O.K., I'll do it!"

When Horace disappeared we were ready. I paid the check and hurried her out. She was giggling nervously as I shut her in the car and trotted around to get behind the wheel.

"Gosh, I never thought I'd do anything like this! He's going to go crazy!"

"Serve him right," I said. I wondered to myself how low a man can get. I felt like the fellow who needed a stepladder to climb under a snake.

My plan was all set. I turned south and made time, the lights of Florence City dwindling behind us.

"Do we have to go so far, Cliff?" she asked. She was sobering fast.

"Just a little farther, Letty."

I turned down Cay Road, down to the deserted strip of beach. I bulled the car through to the packed sand and then drove down the beach, swung toward the moonlit sea, and backed up to the edge of the soft sand. I cut the lights and engine.

"You said, Cliff, that we'd just ride around and cool off. I don't . . ."

She sobbed in her throat as I reached for her. Like a needle stuck on an old cracked record, she said, "No-no-no-no-no . . ." But every vital and muscular ounce of her was saying yes in tones that were twice as loud.

I got out of the car and walked down to the surf line and lit a cigarette with trembling fingers. There is a clean strength about the sea. I felt soiled and old and very tired. Something washed up by the sea. Something that, in order to keep its self-respect, should go drown itself in the clean sea.

When I looked back up the beach at the car she was walking down toward me, smoothing the light blue skirt down over her hips and thighs.

"Well, Cliff," she said in a dead voice.

I lit a second cigarette from mine and handed it to her. She inhaled it deeply and gratefully.

"Take me back, Cliff."

"First we're going to have a little talk about Horace."

"I haven't got anything to tell you. I'm the world's prize damn fool. You haven't been off duty for a minute, have you?"

"I think you better tell me about Horace. I think there's something to tell. It's a hell of a long walk back."

"Then I'll walk," she said flatly.

She turned away. I reached out and caught her by the wrist and yanked her back. "Did you ever think how silly you're going to look, Letty, when he runs out with the dough?"

"What are you trying to say?"

I laughed. "Don't give me that, Letty. Anything but that innocent act. He was afraid you might spoil something yesterday. That's why he slugged you."

She snapped the cigarette into the surf. "I don't know what you're talking about."

"I won't try to ease you out of the cash, Letty. All I want is what they took from Miss Stegman's safe. And if you don't really know what I'm talking about, it's clear proof that Horace is going to ditch you."

She stood very still and stared up at me. The line of her mouth in the moonlight was ugly. "What kind of a trick is this?"

"Please, honey. I'm a big boy now. I know that what I've got on Horace won't stand up in court, but it's plenty good enough for me."

"Are you trying to tell me," she said in a thin high voice, "that Horace was in on . . ."

"As you damn well know," I said.

She was good. She stared out to sea and she covered Horace and all his ancestors in several hundred well-chosen words. When she was through she grabbed the front of my jacket and said, "Believe me! I didn't know anything about it. But now I can see how stupid I've been."

"So fill in on Horace for me."

"He's no good. He never has been any good. He's always got another girl on the string, and when I object, he slaps me around. I don't know why I stay with him. It hurts him to give me a dollar. He got a DD from the army in '44. He's never done time, but he should have. When we were hard up and I was a lot slimmer, he had me picking up men. Then he would bust in and shake them down. He got us the jobs with Miss Stegman by using faked papers and references. When all this happened, I should have guessed right away. I'm going to go back to him and I'm going to tell him that . . ."

"No, you're not," I said firmly. "Use your head. He'll deny everything. If you've been out of it so far, he doesn't want you in on any part of it. The way it shapes up, he steered the thieves onto Miss Stegman for a cut of the proceeds. They haven't been paid off yet by my company, and so Horace hasn't got his cut yet. If he gets ten per cent, it will add up to forty thousand."

Even above the roar of the waves I heard her quick intake of breath.

"And so, Letty," I said, "the last thing I want you to do is to tip him off that I know. And if you go to him after the way we ran out together, he'll guess immediately. I don't want him to be on guard. I like you, Letty. I want to see you get a fair deal out of this."

"But I . . ."

"Look. This is murder. Maybe you don't know the law. If Horace steered them onto her and they killed her, he is just as much a murderer as they are. And don't think he doesn't know that."

That rocked her. I could see it. In a small voice she said, "He has been . . . awful nervous lately."

I had her nicely softened up now for my king-size question. I slipped it across casually. "Where did he go after I saw you people yesterday?"

"Now, that's a funny thing when you think of it, Cliff. He went out by himself. He wouldn't let me come with him. There was gas in the Buick, but he didn't take it. And he hates to walk, that one. He was gone a couple of hours, and when he came back he looked pretty smug about something."

"Letty, you keep an eye on him and you let me know if he does anything you can't understand."

"You won't get him arrested?"

"How about if he runs out on you?"

"Then he can rot!" she screamed.

We walked back up to the car. As I held the door for her she said, "This was a dirty trick, Cliff."

"I know it. I'm in a dirty business."

I went around and got behind the wheel. Her fingers clamped down on my arm. "But you're forgiven, you know."

"Am I?"

"Of course you are." She slid over very close to me, pressing warm against me, her cheek against my shoulder. "Sometimes you learn you've hooked up with the wrong guy, Cliff."

I turned the key and pressed the starter. She reached out and turned the key off again.

"The joint will be closed," I said. "It might be pretty awkward."

Her sigh came from the soles of her sandals. "All right. Let's go."

My watch was a little off. When we got back the Bomb Run was dark and empty. Letty was getting more nervous every moment. Their place, the Belle-Anne Courts, was just a short distance away. I drove up there and parked outside. I reached across her and pressed the handle down to open the door. It swung open slowly and then there was a shadow outside the door and it swung hard the rest of the way.

She didn't make a sound as he dragged her out. I heard the harsh snuff as he breathed out, heard the slapping sound his fist made against her. I went out my side and around the back of the car. They made long shadows across the grass. The nearest street lamp was on the far side of the street.

She did not cry out, merely tried to cover her face. He hit her hard in the belly and I heard the wind hiss out of her. As she doubled over he slammed her behind the ear and she fell to her hands and knees on the grass. He kicked her in the side just as I reached him. I grabbed his shoulder and spun him around.

Horace moved like dark oiled lightning. But there was a deep and tragic flaw in his philosophy of battle. He seemed to believe that a man who stayed on his toes and danced around and swung his fists hard could inflict the most damage. I had that same misconception until one day, in the training area in Scotland, they sent me out to fight a dried-up little sergeant major who must have been over fifty and who weighed not more than 130 in full uniform. By the time we left that area I knew most of his tricks. It's hard to use them properly, as most of them were created with the idea of killing the opponent.

I caught Horace's fist in my cupped hand, turned it so that the back was toward me, and pressed both thumbs against it, my hands locked around it. He grunted and went up on his toes, his back arched. When he was in the proper position of strain, I took my right hand and jabbed him with two knuckles in the triangular opening between the ribs at the top of the solar plexus. As he slumped I caught him by the crotch and the nape of the neck and threw him onto the lawn. He hit heavily and rolled over twice. He wasn't unconscious, but there was no atom of fight left in him.

I helped Letty up. She was still cramped over by the pain in her stomach.

"Remember," I whispered, "it was just a joke. We got stuck in the sand or we'd have been back over an hour ago."

She nodded. When I looked back from the car she was kneeling beside Horace.

I went to an all-night diner and phoned Harry Banson. I knew that if I didn't do it right away, I wouldn't do it at all. I got him at his house. His voice was rusty with sleep.

"Damnit, Cliff, why can't a man . . ."

"Please shut up." Through the glass of the booth door I could see a big table of high-school kids after a dance. They were lifting Cokes off the table and out of sight for the spike job. "Harry, I think this might be a pretty productive night to put a tail on Horace Franklin. If a woman keeps her mouth shut, it might not pan out into anything. But you can't plan on it. And remember, I didn't put you onto this."

"Cliff, is Franklin mixed up in . . ."

"I won't answer any questions, Harry. If you're interested in making a showing, just do what I say. Do it yourself. That'll be best all around. And another thing.

No, never mind the second thing. I'll handle that." I hung up.

I looked up the number and dialed Marty Mennick, our local Cadillac dealer. The phone rang a long time. He answered sleepily.

"Marty? Cliff Bartells."

"Oh," he said. Marty's a political wheel. I'm poison. "What's on your mind?"

"It's none of my business, Marty, but your daughter is down at the Bay Diner with a gang of kids."

"So?" Very cold.

"How old is she? Seventeen? She's got half a load and the boys in the group have a full load. So I'm a snitch. I've unwound too many local kids from around trees and taken too many motors out of too many laps. Personally I think you're a jerk, but that shouldn't stop you from getting down here fast and breaking it up."

I slapped the phone back on the hook, had a cup of coffee at the counter, and then went out and sat in my car. The timing was excellent. Just as the gang came lurching out, Marty came roaring up in his demonstrator. Much loud talk. He shook them free of a set of car keys, loaded them all in, and took off.

It was well after two and time for bed, but there was a restlessness in me. The case was beginning to display a few frayed edges. If I could grab the right thread and pull hard . . . I cruised the night streets. I drove across the causeway bridge to Florence Beach and saw the lights still on in the game rooms at the Kit-Kat, cars still standing in the parking area, glinting under the floods. When I came back off the beach I went by Stackson's Funeral Home. Miss Stegman was in temporary residence there, as that is the only storage vault available to the local police. Even that had an angle. Stackson is a heavy contributor to the party in power, a lodge brother of Powy, a distant relative of Commissioner Guilfarr.

I drove by the Coral Strand. A figure had just walked out of there. There was something familiar about it. As I cruised by I saw that it was Furny Trumbull. I looked back and saw that Melody's light was still on.

I went around a slow block, came back, and parked in the shadows. Aside from a thread of distant music, there was no sound in the night. I drifted across the patch of sand to where I could put a cautious eye to the gap between the venetian blinds and the edge of the window frame. I could not see her. The bed was turned down, but unrumpled. There was a distant hissing sound.

Just as I was about to turn away, the hissing sound stopped. In a moment she came out of the bath, tall and golden, beads of water standing on her body, a towel over her· shoulders. I could hear her humming an old song. As she took a cigarette from the bedside table, I went over and tapped softly on the door.

"It's no use, Furny," she said. "Go away."

"I don't think he's coming back," I said.

"Cliff?"

"Forgive the hour."

"Wait just a moment, Cliff."

She had a thin robe belted around her when she opened the door. She was smoothing damp hair back from her forehead with the back of her hand and she was smiling at me. I looked at her and I thought of the Franklin woman and in some very devious and unexpected way I felt a deep shaft of regret, as though I had cut myself off from this girl on purpose.

"I really won't bite, Cliff. Come in. I've got something to tell you."

She left the door open. I sat on a straight frail chair and she sat on the bed. "The female has made up her mind," she said.

"About?"

"About Furny. It wasn't a fight, I suppose. Oh, we were very calm with each other, but it went on for hours. I feel sort of sorry for him. I guess he really did want to be married to me. But without Aunt Elizabeth backing him up, there doesn't seem to be any point in trying to go through with it."

"How did he take it?"

"Fine, right up to the end. And then he scared me a little. Look at my arm. It's getting blue already." She pulled her sleeve up. It was definitely a bruise that a man's hand might make.

"There was something odd in his eyes, Cliff. It scared me."

"Odd?"

"All the way through he acted as though he were humoring me. You know. Like talking to a child. Telling me what a terrible shock this all was. And then he suddenly realized that I meant it, that I had really decided that I wouldn't marry him, never would marry him. His voice went all funny and his hands shook so that he couldn't light a cigarette. After he hurt my arm he stormed out of here."

She seemed more amazed than frightened. "I guess, Melody, he's always had pretty much his own way. This is a shock to his system."

"Why did you stop by, Cliff?"

"Restless. I didn't like the way our evening ended yesterday."

"It was a good evening and a good ending to it. I wanted to see you anyway. I received a wire from the lawyers this afternoon. Their Mr. Rainey will be here tomorrow morning with all the papers. Maybe you'll want to talk to him."

"I will. He'll be representing you, I suppose. There'll have to be a formal claim presented on the theft policy. What kind of a guy is he?"

"I've never met him, Cliff. It's a good firm. Old line. He's a junior partner or something." She yawned and then gave me a shamefaced smile. "The argument with Furny took a lot out of me, I guess."

She walked with me to the door. As I turned to say good night to her, she put her hand lightly on my shoulder, leaned up, and kissed me on the lips. "Stop looking as though all is lost, Cliff," she whispered.

I went back to my place, showered, and went to bed. But I couldn't sleep for a long time. When I did I had a crazy dream. I was playing shuffleboard. Letty kept flooding the board with beer. Melody stood with Horace's arm around her, laughing.

7

I woke up and the sheets were sodden with perspiration. The hot spell was still continuing. It was strange February weather. Saturday morning. Wednesday morning Arthur had told me of the Stegman death. Wednesday evening I had seen Tony Lavery. Thursday evening in Tampa with Melody. And last night . . . I found that I didn't want to think about last night.

I took a morning shower, and as I turned the water to

cold I invented a new race of men. There would be a
little trap door over the right ear. On mornings after the
people could open the little doors, take out their souls,
and scrub them clean under the shower. It would be
handy. A world full of smiling faces and shining souls . . .

The bathroom radio warned me in stentorian tones of
the state of the world as I shaved. It's odd that there are
so few radios in bathrooms. I won't have one anywhere
else. Most of the advertising is on that level to start with.

". . . inability to find any common points of agreement
with the Russian representatives . . ." he said. ". . . Mid-
west caught in the grip of a new blizzard. Three deaths
so far. Railroads running behind schedules, roads blocked,
air liner feared lost . . ." he said.

I finished the last dark patch under the chin and held
the razor under the cold water.

". . . and on the local front a flash has just come in to
the studio of a new development in the Stegman murder.
The body of Horace Franklin, chauffeur to the late Miss
Stegman, was found at a quarter to nine this morning in
the bay caught in the pilings of the municipal pier. The
body was discovered by two small boys fishing from the
pier. Though no statement has yet been made by Chief
Powy, it is believed that Franklin was killed by repeated
blows on the head with a blunt instrument. Keep tuned
to this station for the latest local and world-wide news,
brought to you through the courtesy of . . ."

I found that I was still holding the razor under the cold
water. I clicked off the radio. It sat on the shelf, ivory-
white and complacent. I cursed it and then I cursed
Harry Banson and then I cursed Horace Franklin for being dead. When I got my breath I cursed myself for
being right in my hunch.

The alcohol in the lotion stung the invisible nicks in
my face. I picked my watch off the shelf. Ten after nine.
The local station had picked the news up quickly. By
now it had been fed into the national news services, and
in afternoon papers all over the country Florence City
would be receiving another chunk of unwanted publi-
city. The local heat would be more searing than ever.
The real-estate gents and the property owners would
be recoiling in righteous horror. To have the public press
implant in the average man's mind a thought pattern
whereby Florence City was synonymous with sudden

death . . . Public servants, feeling the rake of the spurs, would be bucking and plunging desperately.

I suddenly realized that I had to get to Banson and I had to get to him quickly. With somewhat the feeling of an animal trainer entering a cage full of strange cats, I dressed hurriedly, wolfed a hasty breakfast in the diner, and walked the five familiar blocks to police headquarters.

In the Traffic Bureau somebody was complaining loudly and bitterly about a broken meter, and why did he have to pay if the city couldn't keep the meters fixed? Old Sam was lethargically sweeping down the corridor with a wide brush and green compound. He gave me a white-toothed grin.

"Sam, you seen Sergeant Banson?"

"Yassuh. He been in and out all moanin'. Upstairs now, maybe."

I held out a dollar. "Can you tell him to come down to the men's room?"

Sam gave me a hurt look. "I'll tell 'im, Lieutenan', but I doan want no buck."

"Sorry, Sam. You're the only friend I got left in this place."

I shut myself in one of the cubicles in the men's room. Somebody came in and went out. Then another pair of feet came in.

"Cliff?"

I pushed the door open and he stared in at me. He was in uniform for a change. The pale gray shirt was black at the armpits. His mouth had a nervous squeezed-up look, and his sharp Adam's apple kept running up and down his yellow leathery throat.

"Jesus, Cliff! Jesus!" he said.

"Take it easy, Harry. If anybody comes in, you turn and wash your hands and I'll let this door swing shut. First, have you told anybody?"

"I'm going to have to tell somebody, Cliff. Jesus! You don't know. Sooner or later they're going to find out that I was . . ."

"Get this, Harry. You don't have to tell anybody anything. If you do, Harry, I'm going to cross you up good. So help me. I advise you to tail a guy and he turns up dead. How are you going to look? They need a suspect in the can. It can be you as well as me."

He tried to give me the bleak eye. "It wouldn't work," he said. But his voice was thin.

"What happened?"

"After you hung up I wasn't going to go. Then I decided what the hell. I wouldn't be able to get back to sleep anyway. I'd taken one of the sedans home with me, so that made it easier. I parked down from Belle-Anne with the lights out and the motor running. I guess I got there about quarter after two. You know how sleepy a man gets waiting. All of a sudden I heard a starter and then that big Buick comes busting out the drive and swings south with the tires yelling. I stalled the motor and it took me a minute to get going. It looked to me like he turned toward the beach bridge. By the time I got to the corner I couldn't see him anyplace. I cruised around and after a long time I thought I saw the Buick parked close to that Gulf station this side of the bridge. I went by and walked back. I felt the tail pipe. It was still hot. He wasn't anyplace around. I waited for a while and then I went home."

"So you stall the car and he's dead!"

"Lay off, Cliff."

"The municipal pier is a good five hundred yards north of that Gulf station. If you hadn't been too damn sleepy and lazy to walk around . . ."

"Sure. Which way was I going to walk, though? You figure that out."

He was right. I gave him a tired smile. "O.K., Harry. It was just one of those things. I was going to follow him myself, and then I thought it would be better to have somebody in an official capacity in on it. We both made mistakes."

"How did you know there might be trouble?" he demanded.

He turned quickly toward the sink and I let the door swing shut. Heels with metal reinforcements clacked loudly on the tile floor.

"How goes it, Harry?" a heavy voice said. I recognized it as Powy's.

"Ain't this a hell of a morning?" Harry said.

"Maybe it won't be too bad," Powy said. "I'm beginning to get a line on this thing. You ask me, I don't think it's tied up with the Stegman thing at all. That Franklin woman, she won't say nothing, but I find out they went to a beer joint last night and she runs out with some other fella. Now I got an old girl lives across from the Belle-Anne. She tells me there was a hell of a battle out on the grass in front of the place around two o'clock last night. Suppose this Franklin, scrapping over his wife, gets conked too hard and it kills him. Maybe she was beatin' on her hubby's head while the boy friend holds onto him. So they load the body in the car and take it down to where we found it in that gas station. Then they carry him over and toss him in the bay. The tide is going out. But the luck is bad. The tide carries him along and the body hits the pier. Something tells me we crack this one today and we find it's got nothing to do with the old lady's busted head."

"How about the time of death?" Harry asked weakly.

"The guy runs the beer joint says that just as they closed, and that was right at one o'clock, this Franklin was having a hamburg. That's a break. Doc can check the stomach contents and pin it down inside of ten minutes either way. He's working on it now over to Stackson's."

I heard the rush of water as Powy washed his thick hands. Then the heels clacked toward the door and the pneumatic cylinder sighed as the door swung shut.

I pushed my door open again. Harry was kneading his sharp chin with thin yellow fingers.

I came out of the cubicle. "Harry," I said softly, "take good care of yourself. Don't drop dead. I need you. I was the lucky boy who sneaked out with the Franklin woman."

His eyes widened until I could see the red vein network below the iris. "But . . . but . . ."

"Exactly. They'll find out, and when they do, brother, life is going to turn rugged."

"Then don't be a damn fool! Let me tell him where I fit in."

"Save it, Harry. I've got plans."

I walked toward the door. He said, behind me, "Oh . . . Cliff."

"Yes?"

"The letter came this morning. Thought you might like to know. She's healed up, Angela is. She's coming back, but she's got to take it easy." There was a softness in his eyes that I had never seen there before.

"That's good to know, Harry."

I walked out and down the corridor, wanting badly not to meet anybody. My luck was almost good. Gilman was coming up the steps as I went down. He stopped and stared at me.

"Warm enough for you, boy?" I said, showing all my teeth in a grin.

He didn't answer. All the way down the street I felt his eyes on my back.

I phoned the office at the Coral Strand. It took a long sticky five minutes before Melody came onto the line. Her voice seemed to be the only sane thing in all of Florence City. "Oh, Cliff! I was just leaving. Mr. Rainey phoned me a little while ago. He's registered at the Coast Hotel, and I was on my way over to see him. Can you come along?"

"It's only two blocks from here. I'll wait in the lobby."

The Coast Hotel is a very peculiar institution to find in the middle of Florence City. No patios, palms, pools. Just a square red-brick box with plain excellent food, rooms no different than you would find in Buffalo or Cleveland, except for the air conditioning, and a general air of nonresort-town competence.

I sat in the lobby feeling slightly naked without a necktie. I had a fifteen-minute wait before she came in. She saw me the moment I stood up. She wore a black dress, which I suppose was a concession to the death of her aunt, but which merely accentuated the long clean lines of her body, the molten flow of silver-gold hair.

"I need moral support, Cliff," she said. "He's in Five-eleven. He said to come right up."

She jittered nervously on the elevator. I stood close to her. She smiled at me several times, looked quickly away. The corridor carpet muffled our steps.

I knocked at the door and it was opened immediately by a tall man in his early forties. He held himself very erect. He wore a dark suit, and his dark hair, peppered with gray, was worn in a brush cut. His glasses had ponderous dark horn rims and bows.

"Ah, Miss Chance. Do come in." He flashed me a second look of curiosity.

"Mr. Rainey, this is my friend Mr. Bartells. He is also the representative of Security Theft and Accident."

We shook hands, measuring each other. His hand was cool and dry. In the neat small room the air conditioner buzzed quietly. Papers and a portable typewriter stood on a small desk near the windows.

"Do sit down. Allow me to express my sympathy, Miss Chance. This is a very tragic thing."

"Aunt Elizabeth and I did not see eye to eye, Mr. Rainey, but she was my only close relative."

"Of course, of course," he said. He shuffled the papers on the desk. "I am here because her will appoints me, along with Mr. Dent, as coexecutor of her estate. Mr. Dent, as you no doubt know, has been ill for some time." He coughed. "The estate is, as you no doubt realize, quite large." He flushed as though he had said something dirty.

"Do you have some idea of the total value?"

"All told, Miss Chance, it should be in the neighborhood of half a million dollars, estimating property values conservatively."

He flushed again. "I have taken the liberty of giving you the net figure, after all inheritance-tax deductions. Also, I have not figured in the face value of the theft policy. It has been—forgive me—most difficult for us to deal with your aunt during the past several years." He laughed humorlessly. "I suppose as we all grow older we become eccentric. I wished to speak to you confidentially about two matters, Miss Chance."

"Mr. Bartells is a good friend, Mr. Rainey."

He gave me a dubious look. "Ah, so. Despite our protests, Miss Stegman has refused to use checking accounts ever since a bit of trouble with the bank four years ago. Against our advice, she brought fifteen thousand dollars in cash with her to Florida. I rather assume that the money disappeared along with the jewels. She seemed to feel that there was no danger in carrying such a sum with her on a trip. It makes my task as coexecutor very difficult, as checks would give me the basis to arrive at a proper accounting to the court."

He frowned down at his knuckles. "The second matter is a codicil that was added to her will at her request before she came south. A most unfortunate codicil, we feel. I believe that you could break it if you desire. But you must not mention to the other party—ah . . . Mr. Trumbull—that I have given you this advice."

"What does the codicil say?" Melody asked, frowning.

"I am not at liberty to tell you. The will and the codicil must be read by me to you and to Mr. Trumbull at the same time. I haven't been able to contact him yet. The switchboard is trying to locate him for me. I had hoped that I could get him up here so that we could get this matter accomplished. But there are other matters."

We sat patiently while he ruffled the papers again. He seemed to be the perfect example of the completely humorless man. I guessed that the law firm was very happy with him. He made no more concession to Florida than did the Coast Hotel.

"Ah, yes. The matter of the Franklins, Miss Chance. The couple employed by Miss Stegman. The car, naturally, is estate property, and I suggest that it be sold locally. I shall prepare a routine letter of reference and give them, say, two months' pay and their fare back to Boston. I believe we could properly consider that a moral obligation of the estate, and I am certain that the court will not balk at the expenditure. If you agree, I shall make all of the necessary arrangements."

"It's quite all right with me, Mr. Rainey," Melody said.

"If I may interrupt," I said, finding myself adopting Rainey's measured tones, "there will be a slight hitch in that plan. Horace Franklin was murdered last night."

Rainey's mouth sagged open and his eyes bulged. "How—how perfectly dreadful! Who did that?"

"The police are trying to find out."

Melody had a pinched look around the mouth. "Poor little man," she said.

"I find this atmosphere of violence most distressing," Rainey said.

"You are not alone," I told him.

"As for you, Mr. Bartells," he said, "what does your company plan to do?"

"We have a grace period of ninety days before making a settlement. We'll try to recover the stones. If we can't, we'll pay off the face value, of course."

"How was Horace killed?" Melody asked.

"By blows on the head. Then he was thrown into the bay."

Rainey shuddered visibly. He took out a crisp hanky and dabbed his broad forehead. "Our clients seldom . . . seldom . . ." he said, searching for the right word.

"Die violently?" I supplied.

He gave me a grateful glance. "Exactly. I think I had best contact the widow. Maybe, under the circumstances, a letter of reference and . . . ah . . . three months' pay plus her fare north and, of course, the cost of shipping the body to wherever she may wish it shipped?"

"That's for you to decide, Mr. Rainey," Melody said.

The phone beside the bed rang. Rainey reached a long arm over and scooped it up. "Rainey here. Yes? Ah, good morning, Mr. Trumbull. Hope I haven't inconvenienced you. I'm representing the Stegman estate, Mr. Trumbull, and at your and Miss Chance's convenience, I must get you together for the reading of the will. What? Yes, you are mentioned in the will, Mr. Trumbull. Let me see. It is a few minutes after eleven. You could make it by twelve noon? Splendid!"

He held his palm over the mouthpiece after murmuring, "Just one moment." "Miss Chance, would twelve noon be inconvenient?"

"Not at all."

"Then it's all set, Mr. Trumbull. Room Five-eleven at the Coast Hotel. Yes, you may bring a lawyer to represent you. In fact, I strongly advise it. I will be expecting you."

He hung up. "I shall give you the same advice, Miss Chance. We hope, of course, that you will have us represent you in the future, but owing to the oddness of this will, it might be wise if you employed a local attorney until such time as the will is probated."

"I won't need a lawyer. You can tell me what it means."

"I can do that, of course, but . . ."

She stood up and smiled at him. "Then we shall be back at twelve."

I stood up too. Rainey walked us to the door. "Mr. Bartells' presence is not absolutely necessary, you know."

"I know," she said sweetly.

We went down in the elevator. She agreed to coffee in the air-conditioned grillroom. We found a narrow booth for two, upholstered in red leather. I leaned across and held the light for her cigarette.

"Your dependence on me is very touching," I said.

"Goodness! Stop talking like that stuffed pin stripe."

"I'm still curious."

"Then don't blush when I tell you, Cliff. You've got one picture of yourself as how you think you are. I happen to have another. For me, old Hard-as-Nails Bartells is a sort of myth. I like the other guy you keep hidden. Softy Bartells. A very sweet and very dependable guy."

I couldn't answer because the waitress arrived with the pot of coffee.

Then, as I opened my mouth, I saw Kathy walking down toward the booth, her eyes wide and her face pale under her tan.

8

SHE RECOGNIZED me and quickened her pace, arriving at the booth before I could slide out from under the table. She couldn't see Melody until she was right at the booth.

"Cliff! Oh, Cliff, I . . ." she stopped suddenly and the air grew a bit frosty.

"Miss Baron, Miss Chance," I said, standing up. "Sit down, Kathy. I'll get hold of a chair."

"Howdyado," Kathy said quickly. Then she turned immediately to me. "No, Cliff. I can't. It was just luck finding you. Andy thought he saw you coming into the hotel here. Some woman was in the office, crying and carrying on. She was looking for you. Wilma, the darn fool, gave her your address."

"Blonde? A heavy blonde with a long nose?"

"That's the one, Cliff."

"It sounds like Letty Franklin," Melody said.

I frowned at Kathy. "O.K., so she's trying to find me. Why the panic?"

"I'll tell you in private, Cliff."

"You can talk here, Kathy."

She lowered her face and glowered up at me through the excessively long black eyelashes, arching her back in a trick she has so that the high impudent breasts were outthrust against the sheer fabric of her white office blouse. It is a surly and unruly gesture, and in some odd way it gives her the look that French girls have in those photographs of existentialist groups in Paris.

"Tell me, Kathy."

"All right, then. The woman has a gun. She charged by Wilma with her hand in her purse. She went right to your office, and when she reached the door the gun was half out of the bag. Mart nearly swallowed his bridge. Wilma has been grinning like a cat full of fish heads ever since she left the office."

I patted her arm. "Thanks a lot, Kathy. Go on back and don't worry. She won't shoot me. I won't let her."

Kathy pouted up at me for a moment and her eyes were telling me that I was a darn fool to waste time on a blonde when anyone could tell you that a brunette . . .

She turned on a high heel and left, adding that special something to her walk.

I sat down. "A well-furnished office you have, Mr. Bartells," Melody said.

"We try to keep it in shape."

"One warning you, one gunning for you, one trying to get even by giving your address. . . . Aren't *you* the busy little man? Tell me, Cliff. Is it Letty Franklin?" I nodded. "Why is she angry, Cliff?"

"Because her husband is dead."

"Does she think you killed him?"

"No. But she thinks that I managed to maneuver him into a spot where he had to be killed."

She waited a long moment. "And did you?" she whispered.

"Yes. I did." I gave it flat, no explanations.

She shut her eyes for a moment. The closed lids were shadowed. She opened them and looked directly into my eyes. "A girl can be wrong. I've been wrong before. Maybe it *is* Hard-as-Nails Bartells—with no soft spots."

"Maybe it is."

"Take care of yourself, Cliff. You'd better rush off and attend to this little problem of yours. I can see Rainey by myself. I don't really need you."

I found the waitress down near the door onto the street and paid her. The whole setup was pretty queer. With Powy's theory of what had happened, it didn't seem logical for Letty to be wandering around loose, especially with a gun. It would seem more likely that Powy would be asking her some very direct and pointed questions. Who was the guy you run out with, huh? Who was he? Come on. We'll find out anyway. Who was he?

I had a cold feeling in the pit of my stomach. It would be unwise and unhealthy for many reasons to phone

Powy and say, "Look, grab the Franklin woman, she's gunning for me." His only answer would be, "Aha!"

No, I had to get to Letty and I had to talk some sense into her. To do that, I had to keep that gun from going off.

I grew more cautious as I reached the alley beside Western Auto. It is a good trick to be careful and still keep from looking as though you're slinking. There was a fear inside me bordering on superstition. I had to admit that it would be a very pretty sort of poetic justice if, after last night, Letty blasted a few holes in me. When you deserve shooting, you get very gun shy.

When I got to the far end of the alley I slid along the wall and stuck one eye around the edge. My car sat there in the sun. There was no one on the steps. The lock on my door is the kind that takes an expert to pick. I let the breath out of me slowly. It simplified things. If I could be in my apartment when she arrived, it gave me a much better chance of grabbing the gun.

I wasted no time heading for the foot of my stairs. When I was halfway up I saw movement out of the corner of my eye. I turned and saw her, coming out from her hiding spot behind my car. She held a big Colt .45 automatic in her hand. It was pointed at me, and I could have put my finger on the place where the slug would hit.

A moment like that is frozen forever in time and in memory. Every cinder in the small parking area stood out. She was fifteen feet away and about ten feet below me. I could feel the grain of the gray wooden railing under my hand. A .45 makes a hole on the way out the other side that you can bury your fist in. She wore a sun suit just like the other one, but this one was aqua. Her blonde hair was ratty and tangled. Her face was bleared and puffed with weeping so that she looked fifty.

"Now, wait!" I said, and my voice creaked.

I couldn't have picked a worse place. To run down the stairs would bring me closer. I could run to the top and she could take her time. If I slid under the railing I would drop almost in her lap. She looked up at me, foreshortened by the height. Her eyes were like broken stone.

"Stand still for it, you son of a bitch," she said.

"Letty, listen, I didn't . . ."

Her lips slid back away from her teeth and the sun

glinted on a gold filling as the muzzle came up a little farther. It seemed to be aimed at my eyes when it went off. The authoritative blam of the .45 was deepened by the walls of the buildings that surround the parking area.

Death whispered softly by my left cheek and I let myself drop hard, falling up the steps, rolling over tight against the cinder blocks so the target would be smaller. I heard a yell in the distance, mingled with another two shots. The muzzle kick of the big .45 slammed it up so that her third shot went almost straight up into the air. She was biting her underlip now, and I saw her bring the muzzle down. I saw her shut her eyes in the instant of firing and concrete dust bit the back of my neck as the slug slapped the wall inches above my shoulders. This time it was a burst of three, and I began to hope as I let myself slide down the steps, feet first, belly down.

The inexhaustible weapon hammered again and the slug hit the edge of the step my hand was on, stinging my palm. Then she was trying to pull the trigger and I blessed the dead Horace for knowing enough not to keep a full load of eight pushing down on the clip spring. I rolled over and dropped under the railing. I pulled the gun out of her hand and she went heavily down onto her knees, sobbing with great indrawn breaths, the heels of her hands digging into her eye sockets.

The first guy to come arunning gave me a startled look and tried to turn around in midstride and head back the way he had come. He wound his legs up and slid about ten feet on his chest, never taking his eyes off me.

I began to laugh, helplessly, from reaction.

Five minutes later, as they were bundling the two of us into the police sedan with about five hundred people looking on, one of the Kreshak twins, with his white shirt open down to the belt buckle to show off his manly bronze chest, shouldered up and said, close to my ear, "Tony wants you over there. Right away."

"I think I'm busy," I said. "What do you think?"

He gave me a look of disgust. "All he told me to do was tell you."

The stupid driver blasted the siren for the short run back to headquarters. He cowboyed into the drive and swung around in back of headquarters so fast that gravel rattled off the inside of the fender wells.

They herded the two of us into the basement room.

Gowan was the booking sergeant. Powy was there, his thumbs inside his belt, his fingers fanned out across his belly. Gilman stood behind him, figuratively spitting on his knuckles.

"Nice to have you back, Lootenant," Gilman said.

The traffic man, a new one since I left the force, made his report. "I heard the shots. There were seven altogether. Bartells was on the steps going up to his room. The woman had waited for him to show. She shot at him seven times and she missed him every time. From about fifteen feet, too, Chief."

Gowan was scribbling. Powy looked coldly at Letty. "You admit it?"

She had stopped crying. "I admit it. I tried to kill him. I'm sorry I missed him."

"Where'd you get the cannon, Mrs. Franklin?"

"Horace has—had a license to carry it on account of the money and things Miss Stegman carried around. It was in his drawer at the Belle-Anne Courts."

Powy pulled Gilman over and whispered something to him. Gilman trotted off. The silence was heavy until Gilman came back with the nervous proprietor of the Bomb Run, who obviously had been waiting upstairs.

"You see the man?" Powy asked.

The proprietor looked at me and tried to tell me how sorry he was by his expression. "Right there. That one. He took off with that woman around eleven, maybe a little after."

"We'll make up the statement. Drop around tomorrow to sign it, Dennison. You can go now."

Dennison gave me one more regretful look and left. I guess he hated to lose a potential customer.

Powy swung around and glared at Letty. "So it was him, eh? But you couldn't tell me who it was, could you? Why not?"

She looked at me. "I wanted to kill him."

Powy went to her and rested a fat, fatherly hand on her shoulder. "I know, my dear. You wanted to kill him for killing your husband, didn't you? Did you see him do it?"

I could see her get the general drift. And I could see that she liked it.

"I'm not saying."

"You know, Mrs. Franklin, you can be charged with

assault with intent to kill, with carrying a deadly weapon."

She sneered up at him. "Go ahead. Charge me."

Powy nodded to Gowan. "O.K. Book her. Phone county headquarters and have a couple matrons come over and get her. We won't need her testimony anyway."

Powy looked at me with heavy satisfaction. "O.K., Bartells. Take the laces out of your shoes and take off your belt. Empty your pockets. Put everything on the corner of Gowan's desk."

"What's the charge?" I asked, giving him a stupid look.

"Murder, you damn fool!"

"How long can a man get, Chief?"

He colored up. "Nothing's going to help you this time, Bartells. Nothing in this world. We've got witnesses that saw you sweet-talk the Franklin woman and sneak her away from her husband. We got another witness saw you and Franklin mixing it up by the Belle-Anne Courts." He stared reflectively at Letty's sturdy haunches as she stood answering Gowan's questions. "Can't say much for your taste, Bartells, but it's as plain as the nose on her face. You busted him a little too hard."

I didn't like the look on Gilman's face. De Rider had come in and he was standing muttering to Gilman. It was time to stop the game. "You've had your fun," I said, "but you'd better not book me on that charge. Get hold of Harry Banson."

Powy grinned so that he showed his big tombstone teeth. "Smart, aren't you? Harry left a half hour ago. I let him go so he could fly to New Orleans and meet Angela. You know what, Cliff? I think we can get a confession out of you."

They put me in the isolation cell. It's not off the corridor where the tank and the other cells are. Gilman and De Rider took me there. The cell door was open.

"Turn around," Gilman said. I did.

They both inspected me. "Geeze, a lootenant," De Rider said.

"Put your hands up in the air, Lootenant," Gilman ordered.

"I haven't got any belt. I have to . . ."

"Up, up!" he said.

I shrugged and put my hands up. My pants fell down.

"Lootenant, you're indecent," De Rider said. I was standing in the doorway to the cell.

"I don't think he wants to go in the cell," De Rider said. I caught on and started to back up but I wasn't quick enough. Gilman pushed me hard in the chest with both hands. My feet were tangled in the trousers. I went down hard onto the end of my spine on the concrete.

"See you later, Lootenant," Gilman said. The cell door slammed and the bolt snicked over. They stood and gave me a mock salute, and went down the corridor chuckling to each other.

They let me sit for an hour. I wanted a cigarette badly. Then I heard the footsteps and the creak of leather as they came back. "Here we come, Lootenant!" Gilman shouted in falsetto. I remembered the goings-over I'd given him when he had been under me. I remembered the times I'd put De Rider on probation for excessive brutality.

They came in and De Rider was carrying the chair, Gilman the equipment. De Rider thumped the heavy oak chair down.

"Why'd you kill the guy?" Gilman asked. "Over that blonde bag?"

"Don't ask him anything," De Rider said. "Not yet. Hell, he might answer you and spoil the fun."

I told Gilman what he could do to De Rider and vice versa.

Gilman slapped his hands together like a pistol shot. "That's what I want to hear. Promise me, Lootenant. Be tough, will you? Make this a long afternoon."

The oak chair had sturdy arms. Gilman bowed. "Get on the throne, Lootenant."

"Go to hell," I said, hoping they couldn't hear the shake in my voice.

De Rider rushed me back onto the hard bunk and pinned my arms. I tried to writhe free as I saw Gilman hovering over us, the hard rubber sap upraised on the spring handle, looking for the right spot. It came down and the lights thundered out.

I came out of it sitting in the chair. My ankles were tied to the legs. Gilman was tightening the wide leather strap that bound my left forearm to the chair arm. He put his foot against the seat of the chair at the side in order to get leverage.

"Take a look at that face," De Rider said. "How are they going to tell if we marked him up or not?"

"How they can go for a face like that, I don't see."

"Do you have to be pretty to grab something like that Franklin squab?"

"Me, I was thinking of the dolly in the office. Now, there is something. And did you see the way the Chance girl took off for Tampa with him?"

"I'll be out of here sometime," I said. "Sometime I'll get you two."

"Talk big, Lootenant." Gilman stepped back. "That's tight enough."

"Me first?" De Rider asked.

"Go ahead. You bring the water bucket? I'll get it."

They had spun the chair around so that it faced the bunk. De Rider put the night stick on his lap and carefully rolled it in the big bath towel. He said, "This doesn't leave any marks, Lootenant. I think you were the guy told me it makes pin-point concussions on the surface of the brain, whatever the hell that means."

He smiled at me, leaned over, and hit me squarely on top of the head with the padded night stick. I could feel the thud down to my heels. The room made one wild dip and steadied. My mouth had that numb feeling that comes when you get close to the edge of consciousness.

He grinned and belted me over the ear with it. The blackout lasted a fraction of a second. "You can talk any time, Lootenant."

I grinned at him. "You poor dumb bastard," I said softly. He swung and the lights went out. I woke up as the water slapped me in the face. I gasped for air.

De Rider and Gilman sat side by side, staring soberly at me. Gilman put the dipper back in the water bucket.

He took the wrapped night stick. "My girl told me the other night on the dance floor that I got a wonderful sense of rhythm. Look at here."

I shut my eyes. The old ryhthm. Shave and a hair cut, two bits. The last thud drove me close to blackness again. There was a dull ache deep in my brain.

Then I was trying to tell them that they could ruin a man's mind permanently. They nodded and agreed with me and kept belting me with the stick. I began to lose track of the times they threw water on me. Their faces and pale eyes floated in front of me and there wasn't any sense in the words they said. There wasn't any sense in anything. They beamed and nodded and the brain in my skull was a soft jelly that seemed to smash outward against my eardrums with each blow.

I thought I had felt anger before. Like every man, I had had my moments of wild red rage. But the thing growing in my heart was something new. It had a hard core of ice. It had a color. Steel blue. It had an angular shape, with broken edges. It told me that someday I would get my hands on the throats of Gilman and De Rider. It told me that once I had my hands on a thick throat, nothing would stop the pressure until they cut my hands off at the wrists.

And then the blue anger told me to be sly. I kept my chin on my chest while four dippers of water struck my face. My mind cleared a little.

"He isn't out. He's faking," one of them said.

Hard fingers pinched down on the end of my nose and twisted. The blue anger helped me bear the pain though tears ran from the corners of my closed eyes. I heard a match strike.

"If he's faking, this'll bring him out of it."

There was an area of heat on the back of my hand. It sharpened and deepened and the blue anger helped me hold my hand there, limp and lax. As the heat deepened it turned into a pain that could not be distinguished from cold. It was as though an icicle were being pressed slowly down through my flesh.

I could smell the sick taint of burned flesh.

"Softer than I thought," one of them said. The other cursed. Deep inside me something was laughing.

The straps loosened. I made myself stay limp as I slid out of the chair. My mouth hit the concrete and I tasted blood. There was a scraping sound and the clang of the door and footsteps receding. I waited a long time before I moved. Then I crawled to the water bucket they had left. It was half full. On my knees, I thrust my head down into it, the displaced water rising until it covered my face. Three times I did that and then I had the strength to pull myself up onto the bunk. It seemed as high as a ten-foot wall.

A man cannot be knocked unconscious without a severe shock to his nervous system. There was no specific point of soreness on my skull. It felt as though the solid bone had been pulped. I lay on my back and pressed my hands to my temples and tried to think clearly. Even memory was disjointed and confused. Cumulative shock had given me the feeling of madness.

But the blue anger was there. It was too big for just De Rider and Gilman. It was big enough to fit around those two and Powy and Guilfarr and Lavery. It was big enough to fit around every self-righteous fat-gut crooked official in the county.

I lay there and thought of the Laverys, the syndicate boys. They sell a good story. Leave us alone and you'll have a clean town. We'll help you keep it clean. No trouble. The mobs don't gun each other any more. There's enough for everybody. So a cop sees the white beaches and the expensive blondes and the six-thousand-dollar convertibles, and he thinks about his $3,180 a year and the mortgage payments and braces for Nancy's teeth. A nice clean fifty rustles when you fold it up. So when they tell you to frame some scared kid, what can you do? Are you a Christer cop like Bartells? Look what happened to him. No, you've pocketed the payoffs, Copper. Now earn your change. Make Florence City safe for the crooked wheels and sticky dice and edged decks. Everybody's grabbing theirs. Don't be a sucker too. Grab yours now—while it's hot. But don't forget where it comes from, Copper.

9

POWY WOKE ME up by shaking me. "On your feet, Bartells."

I sat up, slapping his hand away. The pain in my head wasn't so bad, but I was as shaky as though I were coming out of a long illness. My eyes were grainy and my tongue was thick and furred.

He threw my personal belongings on the bunk beside me.

I stared up at him. "How come?"

"Never mind how come. You're out."

His small eyes were blazing and his color was high. I knew he was sore about it, but that it was something he had to do.

"How come you're doing something intelligent, you fat fud?"

"God damn that mouth of yours, Bartells!"

"How did that peanut brain ever discover that I didn't kill Horace?"

"You killed him, all right," he said huskily. "You're guilty as hell. Everybody has gone crazy. Tony ought to know that . . ." His mouth clamped shut.

I laughed at him. "Tony says let me go and you have to let me go. That's great. Suppose Tony told you to burn down the building, Fatty?"

He controlled himself with an effort. "I'm supposed to tell you that Tony wants to see you just as soon as you can get over there."

I picked my wrist watch out of the brown manila envelope with my name on it and strapped it on. It was a quarter after two. That shocked me a little. I expected it to be nearly dusk.

"Come on, come on," he said impatiently.

I stood up and I had to put a hand out and brace myself until the wave of dizziness wore off. I looked down into his face. "Powy, you turned me over to Gilman and De Rider. I'm not going to forget that. Ever."

He backed up a little and snorted. "You aren't scaring me, Bartells."

"What did Doc say about the time of death?"

"I guess it won't help you any to know. Three o'clock, give or take ten minutes."

I thought back. It had been just about three when I unlocked my door. I had left Melody at about quarter of. According to Harry, Franklin had driven out at probably twenty after two. The gas station was a five-minute drive from the Belle-Anne Courts. It would fit. A little conversation with the man or men who had killed Aunt Liz, and then *boom*.

I pulled my belt tight. "Ready."

He had me walk ahead of him through the steel door and along the tier of cells and out into the corridor that led to the front door.

"Remember, Tony wants you to . . ."

I cocked my head on one side. "Shut up a minute." I listened. I had been right. It was a very familiar voice and it took only a moment to learn that it was coming over the transom of the nearest closed door.

I turned the knob and yanked the door open. Melody was sitting very straight and very pale beside Powy's desk. Gilman had a heavy hip balanced on one corner of the desk and he was bending over her, talking right down into her face.

"You can't say that sort . . ." Melody said angrily. She broke off as she saw me. Gilman turned around with a startled expression.

Powy edged by me as Melody stood up and moved away from Gilman. "What goes on here?" he demanded.

I was very proud of Melody. She put her chin up and there was ice in her voice. "I might ask you the same thing, Chief Powy. The other day you gave me the impression that you are anxious to find who killed my aunt."

"Why, I certainly am, Miss Chance," he said.

"Don't let her smoke-screen you, Chief," Gilman said with a faint sneer in his tone.

"Will you kindly ask that—that officer to be still?" Melody said.

"Shut up, Gil," Powy rumbled. Gilman shrugged.

"If what you are doing about the death of my aunt's chauffeur is any indication of how sincere you were . . ."

"Would you get to the point, Miss Chance?"

I saw the blush creeping up her slender throat. "I found out you arrested Mr. Bartells for murder, Chief Powy."

"So?"

"So Mr. Bartells couldn't possibly have killed Horace Franklin."

I couldn't decide what she was driving at. I must have worn a stupid look. She gave me a warning glance.

"Just how do you figure that?" Powy said, using his fatherly tone.

"Mr. Bartells was with me."

Powy pursed his lips. "With you? Now, that's interesting. Just how would you happen to know the time of death, Miss Chance?"

She stared into space over the Chief's head. "Horace Franklin was killed sometime during the night, wasn't he?" she asked softly.

We all realized what she was driving at at the same moment. Powy's attitude up until that point had been quietly respectful, fatherly. He gave me a look of grudging respect.

Gilman said, "That's what she was telling me, Chief. So I was trying my luck. All they can do is say no."

I found my tongue. "Nice try, Melody. But it won't work. Besides, there's no point in it. They're letting me go."

"Don't try to protect me, Cliff," she said.

Powy stared at her. "You never can tell, can you?" he said heavily.

I turned toward him. "Damnit, she's lost her marbles. Check on it. Look. Get hold of Marty Mennick. Ask him what time I called him last night, and from where."

Powy looked confused. Gilman grinned, moved closer to Melody, and muttered something that only she could hear. Her hand flashed around and her palm bounced off his hard cheek. She walked toward me with precarious dignity. "Will you take me home, please, Cliff?"

I took her by the elbow. "A pleasure," I said.

We went out the door before Powy could decide what to do. I hurried her down the corridor and down the wide stone steps in front. She dug her car keys out of her purse and said, "I parked over there, Cliff. By the drugstore."

The windows were up and the little gray Chevvy was like a Dutch oven inside. As I started the motor I looked across the street and saw Gilman standing at the top of the steps, still grinning, as he watched us.

I yanked the little car out into traffic and gunned it down to the corner, barely beating the light.

Down near the causeway bridge there is a parking space on the bay shore where some old trees, bearded with gray moss, give shade. She didn't object as I turned into the parking space and parked in the shade. We both got out of the car. I walked around and took the cigarette pack out of her hand, and held a light for both of us. She inhaled deeply and shuddered slightly as she exhaled. Her hand trembled as she took the cigarette from her lips.

"A great act," I said. "Maybe Metro will buy it."

"Shut up," she said wearily.

"Lovely heiress slanders self to free accused. No. They won't buy it. It's too fresh off the cob."

"Will you *please* shut up?"

"One thing baffles me a little, Miss Chance. How do you know I didn't help Horace into his reward?"

The eyes went wide and they looked greener than I had seen them before. "But you told me you didn't!"

I laughed. I couldn't help it. "I give up. I really give up."

"After what happened, I had to find you, Cliff." She turned away from me and looked out across the bay. All I could see of her face was the bold curve of the left cheekbone, the dark tip of an eyebrow, the rounded tip of her nose.

"Call me Chloe."

She whirled around and there was gray lightning in her eyes. "What's happened to you? What did they do to you in there?"

Inadvertently I looked down at the back of my hand. She followed the direction of my glance and I heard her sharp intake of breath. The act of driving had broken the crust that had formed across the deep burn. "Oh," she said softly. She went to the glove compartment and came back with a small first-aid kit in a khaki case. She put it on top of the hood and opened it. "Hold your hand out, Cliff." The ointment was cool and pleasant. The little gauze pad covered the place, and the two strips of adhesive held it down.

She tried to smile. "Don't tell me they burned you?" she said scoffingly.

I could have said no. But I was the small boy on the schoolyard showing his scars to the girl in the blue hair ribbon. I was chinning myself on the low branch of the apple tree. I was diving into the old quarry from the highest rock.

So I let her read the answer in my eyes. "But, Cliff! That sort of thing—it just doesn't happen! My God, this isn't Spain at the time of the Inquisition!"

"Wake up!" I said. "Take a good look around. Do you believe everything you read in the newspapers?"

"Those men—they ought to be punished, Cliff. People ought to know about things like this."

"Sure. I'll make out a notarized statement. Do you think it'll hit the front page? Do you think I'll get a medal? Nuts, Melody. I can't prove anything."

A breeze off the bay stirred the hem of her black dress. "Cliff, I had to get you out of there. Any way I could. There's nobody else."

"I'm surprised you've stayed out of trouble this long, the way you go around trusting people."

"If I'm wrong this time, I'll find out sooner or later.

Listen to me, Cliff. We had the little meeting in Mr. Rainey's room. He read the will as though it hurt his mouth. The codicil is very peculiar. I can't tell you the legal way it was written, but here's what it says: I'm to get an income of four hundred a month until I marry Furny. Then I get the whole estate. If I don't marry him and don't marry anyone, I get the four hundred a month for the rest of my life, and when I die, the estate goes to Furny if he's still living. If he has married and has died, the estate goes to his heirs. If he has died without marrying, the estate reverts to the State of Massachusetts. If I marry someone else, the income ceases until my oldest child is twenty-one. A trust fund is established that will give each child a hundred dollars a month for life when he or she reaches twenty-one. After the trust funds are set up, the balance of the estate goes to Furny, or his heirs or the State of Massachusetts, as the case may be at that time."

"How did Trumbull act?"

"He was nervous at first, and still very annoyed with me. He brought along a young loud-mouthed lawyer. Then when he found out what the codicil meant, he began to look so terribly smug. He leaned back in the chair and beamed."

"I can see why Rainey felt that the will could be broken. I don't think that a will can be set up in such a way as to coerce you into marrying a specific person. It can have different arrangements in case you marry anybody or stay single, but I don't think that it can be set up the way she has it and stick."

"From the way Furny's lawyer acted, I think you're right. But all that isn't important. The conference was short and I left at about twenty after twelve. I had a quick lunch downstairs, and I was worrying about you and that woman. I decided to go back and change before finding out what happened to you. I went into my room and it was just like I had left it. That horrible woman hadn't cleaned up yet. Right on the floor, almost under the bed, there was a ring."

Her lips had begun to tremble. I took hold of her hands. "Take it easy, Melody."

"That's why I've been so frightened, Cliff. So desperately frightened. That's why I went down there when I found out they were holding you and tried to get you

out. It was one of Aunt Elizabeth's favorites. A good
star ruby in an antique gold setting."

"Where is it?"

"I—I left it there. I just happened to see it by accident
just as I was about to take my dress off. I stood for a
long time staring at it, and just the thought of having it
there in my room made me feel as if I couldn't breathe. I
listened and I couldn't hear any sound anywhere. So I
ran, Cliff. I ran."

It made no sense to me. I even looked at her to see if
there was any evidence that she was faking her fear.

"You left the ring there?"

"I didn't touch it, Cliff."

"Come on, then. Get in the car."

I ran two lights getting there, while other cars honked
indignantly. She sat with her hands locked in her lap,
staring straight ahead. I pulled into the rutted drive of
the Coral Strand and nosed in to a stop near her door.

Her door was open. "Did you leave it that way?
Open?"

"I—I can't remember."

I went ahead of her. Through the screen, in the dimness of the room, I could make out somebody sitting on
the unmade bed, a dark shadow against the sheets.

I pushed the door open. Furness Trumbull gave me a
thin-lipped smile. Melody came in behind me. "What are
you doing in here, Furny?"

"Waiting for you, my dear."

"How did you get in?" I asked him.

"I'll pretend you have the right to ask, Bartells. I do
have the name right? The old woman took pity on me.
It was hot there in the sun. She lent me the extra key."

"For a consideration," Melody said casually. She
walked over toward the bureau. I could see that she was
trying to get to an angle where she could inconspic-
uously look behind Furny's legs.

He turned blandly and watched her. She bent over so
that she could see her reflection in the low mirror. She
smoothed a strand of hair back over her right ear. "Do
we have anything to talk about, Furny?" she asked.

"I suppose your *dear* friend Bartells must share these
tender moments?"

"Of course."

"I think I would have insisted that he stay anyway, my

dear. You see, I am in somewhat of a state of shock. I've been sitting here, trying to make sense of everything."

"You can't quite believe that I'm still saying no?" she asked, acid-sweet.

"Well, you did make it rather humiliatingly evident in front of Mr. Rainey and Mr. Barkaw. Let me see if I can quote you exactly. 'I'll be quite satisfied with four hundred a month from now on.'"

"Why did you come here, Furny?"

"Since coming, I've changed my mind. Originally I came to try to make a compromise. Since you find me so distasteful since Elizabeth died, I thought we might be married here. I would leave immediately for the North and you could stay here and establish residence and get a Florida divorce. It's quite simple, they tell me. I would promise not to make any attempt to exercise my prerogatives as husband. That would satisfy the codicil. I thought that it would be worth a hundred thousand to you to get your hands on four hundred thousand. I didn't think I was being too greedy. What do you think, Mr. Bartells?"

I glanced over at Melody. From the way she held her mouth I knew that she had taken a good look under the bed when Furny had turned to me. And I knew that the ring was no longer there.

"If you've changed your mind about suggesting the compromise, Trumbull," I said, "then the question is pretty academic, isn't it?"

He leaned back across the bed, his elbows behind him, propped up at an angle. "This is a *dreadful* foom, Melly."

She walked to the edge of the bed, looking down at him. "Come on, Furny. I know you very well. You're a poor poker player. What is it?"

He no longer smiled. "There have been certain things that I haven't understood. They have puzzled me. Little things, Melody. This sudden great friendship for—for a small-time insurance adjuster. Your refusing to live with Elizabeth. I suppose most of us are pretty dense when we come face to face with this sort of situation. The blonde, the booty, and the small-town crook. Neither of you, by yourselves, would have the guts to go through with it, I imagine. But Mr. James M. Cain has enlightened us on the false courage that an illicit affair gives a pair of fools, hasn't he? Remember *Double In-*

demnity? I always suspected you of having a savage streak, Melody. How did you work it? I can imagine. Elizabeth would have opened the door for you, Melly. You could have put it off the latch for your friend here. I rather imagine he struck the blow. He has that look, you know. Maybe you don't see it now. I think you'll see it later, after you've had a chance to get a little weary of each other."

"Just what are you trying to say?" Melody asked.

He brought one hand around in front of him and opened his fist. The blood-red stone lay on his broad palm. It picked up a shard of light from the window.

"So careless of you, dear," he whispered.

"I came back here and I found it on the floor! I came back here and found it!" Her voice was thin.

"Of course you did. Poor Elizabeth. She died between midnight and two. And I knew that *you,* Melly, couldn't have done such a terrible thing, so I was gallant. I forgot to mention the little quarrel we had. I told them that we were together until four in the morning and you told me that was very decent of me."

She backed away from him. "But I told you! I walked on the beach. I walked and walked until I was exhausted. Furny, you can't possibly . . ."

I took her gently by the shoulders and turned her around. Her eyes were wide and wild. "Easy," I said. "Easy! Let him make his offer."

"Now you're talking sense," Trumbull said. "I'm not a fool, and I don't intend to be quixotic. Elizabeth was a dear friend, but she's dead, and punishing you, Melly, won't bring her back to life. I'm a reasonable sort. But now I don't have to plead any more. I think we'd better get married. It will be the same arrangement as I suggested before, but with one slight change."

"What's that?" I asked.

"Half," he said. "A full half."

"Or?"

"Or I regretfully go to the police and give them this ring and tell them where I found it. I then explain why I lied about Melody's being with me that evening. I'm certain they'll appreciate how clever it all is. The one man who can most safely profit from the theft of the stones is the man empowered to buy them back in the name of the company. And it will be easy to prove that you, Melody, knew nothing of the codicil to the will until today. That must have been a rude shock."

She put her hands to the sides of her head. "This is all crazy!"

"Elizabeth showed me a few of those letters you wrote her when you returned gifts she sent you, Melody. I saved a few of them."

"Go and take a walk, Melody," I said.

She held tightly to my arm. "No, Cliff. That won't help. We've got to make him see that this is absurd."

I smiled at her. "Give up, baby. He's got us. Let's not be greedy. There's enough for everybody."

Furny's eyes widened momentarily. He said, "That's a sane attitude."

"So let's not pressure each other," I said, "or somebody will get excited and make mistakes. She can't marry you this minute, you know. Give it a few days. But we'll have to be able to trust you, Furny. At the time of her marriage we'll want the arrangement written out and signed by all three of us, just in case. She'll settle half the estate on you."

Melody began to laugh. It climbed into hysteria, the tears squeezing out of her eyes. I slapped her out of it. The aching sounds stopped abruptly. She moved slowly away from me, backing up step by step, staring at me as though I were something incredibly evil. Oddly enough, she had never looked more lovely than she did at that moment.

"Naughty, naughty," a voice with a faint suggestion of a lisp said from just outside the screen door. "Slapping women."

Harry and Larry Kreshak stood looking in at us.

"Will you come along nice?" Larry asked. "Tony's real upset. You're making him nervous." They shouldered their way in. "He's beginning to think you're avoiding him." Hands clamped on my arms above the elbows, numbing my fingers. "Come nice, laddy."

10

THE CREAM-COLORED Cadillac was parked down in front of the office. The greasy female Buddha stood squinting in the sun, staring up at the three of us.

"Get your hands off me," I said.

"Now, laddy. We're just a couple of aging beach boys trying to get along."

I tried to make my tone reasonable. "Look. I don't want to leave the girl back there with Trumbull. I'll come right along."

"Tony said to bring you, Bartells. He didn't say urge you."

We approached the car. The motor was purring softly. The top was down and the boot on. With the two hands on me, I couldn't move. But I knew that one of them was going to have to let go of me to put me in the car. I had taken enough pushing around for one day—for the rest of my life, if it came to that.

Larry was on my left. They walked me up to the right-hand door. Larry opened the door and let go as Harry shoved me into the seat. I brought my left arm around and stabbed at Harry's eyes with my spread fingers. He was quick enough to see it coming, and he let go of my arm and dodged back. I slid across the seat, slapping the gear arm up, stamping on the gas with my left foot before I had hold of the wheel.

Larry was trying to swarm in after me as the big cream-colored car leaped backward. The open door knocked him flat as the old lady screamed. I got behind the wheel and got the automatic shift arm into the right position. Larry was picking himself up, spitting sand, and Harry was running toward the car. I swung it toward him and he changed his mind. He turned and tried to run across toward the high hedge on the other side. The big car rocked after him and he started screaming as he ran. The rear wheels spun in the sand. He tried to cut to the side when he was still five steps ahead of me. I swung toward him, got him centered, and then swung hard right just as I made contact. The front left fender bunted him squarely in the seat of the tailored slacks. He pinwheeled once in the air before he hit the top of the hedge. I jammed on the brakes with the nose of the car buried in the hedge as I heard the sick thud he made as he struck the stucco back wall of the neighboring tourist court.

I backed the car in a tight spin and saw that Larry was standing transfixed, his face greenish under his tan. Beyond him and off to my left, Melody stood with her hands at her throat, Trumbull in the doorway behind her.

"Don't, Cliff!" I heard her scream over the roar of the motor as I started toward Larry. He broke out of his trance, spun around and ran for Melody's coupé. He yanked the door open and clawed his way inside, yanking the door shut, sobbing aloud with fright.

He stared bug-eyed at me as I eased the Cadillac up to the side of the coupé. I put the bumper against it and gunned the motor. The coupé slid and then rocked up. Larry's face disappeared. The coupé balanced for a moment on two wheels and then went over onto its side with a crash.

I opened the side door. "Get in here!" I yelled to Melody. She stared at me with the dull and uncomprehending look of someone who, for the first time, witnesses madness.

I do not think that she would have come to the car if Trumbull had not stepped forward and put his arm around her. The reason why marriage was impossible for them was immediately evident. The corners of her mouth went up in the semismile that comes from an unpleasant taste. The shudder of distaste rippled up through her and she moved forward out of the bend of his arm.

"Get in the car," I said, fighting for a conversational tone. I could hear the excited voice of the woman manager. "Police! Quick, police!" she was yelling into the phone.

Melody came to me then, half running, breathing through her parted lips while Trumbull scowled. She pulled the door shut and I backed around and headed out toward the street. I glanced in the rear-vision mirror and saw Larry standing inside the coupé, his head and shoulders protruding from the open window, blood on his forehead, his cheek, and the shoulder of the white shirt.

I raced through the back streets to the causeway bridge. My luck was bad. The red lights were flashing and the siren was sounding and the floor of the bridge was lifting to let a charter boat through, the outriggers lashed high.

I stopped behind the car ahead of me and another car boxed me in as the line formed. She was as far away from me as she could get, her right side pressing against the door. She wouldn't look at me.

My hands were shaking with reaction. The bandage she had applied was loose, folded back. I pressed it over into place.

"Why did you say those terrible things to Furny? About us?"

I wanted to laugh. Try to guess a woman's reactions. She saw me use the car as a weapon to smash the Kreshak twins. But that wasn't the thing on the top of her mind. The important item was my faking with Furny.

"I wanted to give us time, damn it. I wanted to get him out of there. I wanted time to think. Nothing seems to be making sense any more. Nobody is giving me time to think."

Then she looked at me. She ran the tip of her tongue along her lower lip. "Did you kill that man?"

"I don't think so. I could see him through the hedge. He was trying to get up onto his hands and knees."

"Why did you insist I come with you?"

"Later, later," I said, as the line started. As we came off the bridge I could see the rambling dusty-pink establishment on the fill out into the bay. I turned left on Beach Road and swung in toward the gate. The gate-keeper, recognizing the Cadillac, swung the gate wide, then stood and stared blankly at me behind the wheel. He shouted weakly after I was by him. I parked it where Tony usually left it, at the point nearest to his office and apartment.

She came hesitantly around the car and I took her by the wrist and pulled her along with me as I went in. Tony was coming out of his office. He stopped and stared.

He smiled with a noticeable lack of enthusiasm. "You're an ungrateful guy, baby. The longer I know you, the more you bother me. Who's your friend?"

I had to get to him quick without the usual pleasantries. I didn't have time to worry about hurting Melody's feelings.

"This is Miss Chance, Tony, and she is half a million bucks on the hoof, so watch your manners and invite us in."

Tony put on graciousness like a tailored jacket. "Please don't let my crude friend disturb you, Miss Chance. My name is Lavery and they tell me I'm running this fun house, though sometimes I wonder. Won't you please come in?"

He held the door wide and closed it behind us. He ushered Melody to a deep chair by the windows with all the unctuous charm of a shoe salesman fitting a size 5AA to a 6B foot.

He drifted toward his little bar. "Miss Chance, I'm glad of this opportunity to tell you that this distressing crime is not at all typical of our community, and . . ."

I took a cigarette off his desk. "Drop the propaganda, Tony. I brought her here to make a certain point. You had me released. Thanks. I couldn't come running because she was in trouble. Very bad trouble. I didn't have a chance to phone you. You got too impatient. Your boys came to cart me away when I was being useful. They wouldn't listen when I talked nice. I think you're going to get a phone call about them pretty soon."

He stood very still with his fingertips on the neck of a bottle. "I wondered where they could be. I was about to ask."

"One of them is probably on the way to the hospital, Tony."

He looked at me for long seconds. When he spoke his voice had the sound of a fingernail being pulled across silk. "That was a good trick. How did you do it?"

"I took your car and ran them down."

It was the first time I had ever seen Tony rattled. He ran his thumb along the little crisp blond mustache. "My God, you didn't horse around, did you?"

"They wouldn't listen to me."

He pulled himself together. "Believe me, Bartells. Please believe me. What you were trying to say to them must have been pretty important. It will have to be pretty important. Five years it took me to bring those boys along."

"If I didn't figure you as smart enough to see my reason, I wouldn't be here. If they took me with them, it would have left Miss Chance alone with Mr. Trumbull. Today Mr. Trumbull found out that Miss Chance gets the Stegman money. He found out that if Miss Chance should die all of a sudden, Mr. Trumbull gets the Stegman money. That wouldn't be important except for one thing: Mr. Trumbull was putting on a funny act for the two of us. There are several ways you can make sense out of his act. One way would be to assume that he was setting the stage in such a way that if Miss

Chance should do away with herself, he would have some good reasons to present to the authorities for her action."

Melody gasped. "But Cliff, I don't think . . ."

"You haven't had time to think. Look how it fits. Yes, I found this ring in Melody's room. I couldn't believe my eyes. I knew it was Elizabeth's ring. I faced her with it. She denied it. I told her that it was my duty to make a complete report to the authorities. Naturally, I never thought that as soon as I left her she would hang herself —or cut her own throat or whatever other way he happened to figure out. Use your head. In Rainey's room you made it pretty clear that in spite of the codicil, you wouldn't marry him. You went to lunch. Where did he go? I say he went to your room and planted the ring. I don't know where he got it. I bet that a little pressure on that old hag landlady will bring out that he was there twice. It gave him a chance to pressure you, and if that didn't work, it gave him a safe basis for killing you, provided he could make it look like suicide."

She began to look angry. "Now, see here! That sounds good, but even though I don't really like him, I don't think he's a fool. He wouldn't dare do anything . . ."

Tony stepped in unexpectedly. "In my business, girl, I get a big chance to see how people react when faced with a large bundle. The smartest people do very surprising things. Besides, I've got an angle on Trumbull. That's why I wanted to see Cliff. I didn't want to give the angle to Powy because every week I fire help who are smarter than Powy is. Suppose you hear my angle and then tell me what you think of this Trumbull?"

Just as Melody nodded, the phone rang. Lavery picked it up. The voice on the other end of the line was loud and excited.

"Hold on!" Tony said. "Wait a minute! Hold on!" He flushed and lost patience. "Shut up!" The voice on the other end of the line stopped. Tony took a deep breath. "Now let me tell you something, Larry. I know all that. He's right here, with the girl. Yes, he came directly here. Now get this. Tell Powy there's no charges." The voice began yapping again. Tony smiled at me and shrugged. The voice faded away. "No charges, Larry. That's an order. And don't act so damn outraged. If you'd used your heads you wouldn't have had trouble. How bad is he?"

He listened for a moment, cupped his hand over the mouthpiece, and said, "Mild concussion and a broken shoulder. Larry's just got a head laceration. They've stitched it already."

He spoke into the phone. "Get on over here. And stop trying to advise me. No, we're not going to do anything." He slammed the phone down.

"They aren't going to be very fond of you, Cliff."

"I think I can stand it."

"Now here's the thing I wanted to tell you. This Trumbull went to one of the syndicate clubs in the North early in January. He had a bad night and he paid off with a very rubbery check. Then he left town and came down here. Things like that are routine. I got the information on him with my orders to go jack him up a little and make a collection if possible. I've been short-handed and I couldn't get around to it. This morning I got word that I could drop it, that they'd received payment in full and a note of apology. Don't things begin to hang together a little better?"

"Why are you telling me this?" I asked.

He gave me a look of weary patience. "Sometimes you're bright. Sometimes you sound like Powy. We had a little talk a few days ago, friend. At that time it looked like you were plunk in the middle. If you tried to buy back the stones, Powy and his boys would stomp you raggedy. If you crossed up a pro outfit, it would be the last recovery you'd ever make. Word gets around fast. Now I come up with a pretty hot indication that it may have been amateur talent all along, a fellow made nervous by giving a bad check to the wrong people. It gives you a nice out. You can make your recovery, double-cross the amateur, and everybody is happy."

"I can follow that, Tony. I'm not that stupid. What I mean is why not hand it right over to Guilfarr and Powy?"

He gave a wary glance toward Melody. She seemed to be lost in her own thoughts. And she had an expression as though she were staring into a chamber of horrors.

Tony lowered his voice. "I'm a businessman and I represent businessmen, Cliff. We take the long view. I told you how certain towns are known as being safe for the Big Rich. Creaming the guy who did it won't be enough. We want a recovery of the stolen goods also.

Guilfarr and Powy could have a shorter view of the whole thing. I'm afraid that they would figure on a conviction as being enough. I'm afraid that if they stepped in, they might develop sticky fingers if they should run across the items that came out of the old lady's safe. They have enough contacts so that they could take it easy and fence the stuff over a period of years. We could stop that if we knew it was true, but we might never find out. And if Trumbull could crab their act by his testimony, Trumbull would be shot in an escape attempt, as you damn well know, and story would be that he died before revealing where he had hid the stones."

"What would I get out of it from you?" I asked.

"If we like the way it's worked out, we'll be generous." He turned to her. "Miss Chance, would you care for a drink? Martini? And how about you, Cliff?"

I looked at his desk clock. Four-thirty-five. A long day. I hadn't eaten since breakfast. "I'll settle for a steak sandwich."

He phoned the order to the kitchen and the room was quiet while he busied himself with the gin, vermouth, and ice.

"What happens to people?" Melody asked.

We both looked at her. "How so?" Tony asked.

"His boat had white sails and it was the most beautiful thing in the whole world. He was thin and brown and he had a nice grin. I suppose he was a kind of hero to me, a boy who went out of his way to be nice to a small girl. When she'd heel over and the sails would snap tight, I'd be scared and I'd hold tight to the edge of the cockpit, but he'd laugh and I remember how white his teeth were against the tan. I remember how blue the water was, and the sound of it against the bow."

Tony gave me a puzzled look. I said, "She knew Trumbull when she was a kid."

He brought her her drink. He stood by her chair and sipped his own and said, "Nobody knows what happens to people, Miss Chance. Take me. Know what I was going to be? An architect. Hell, I was going to build the biggest damn shining buildings you ever saw. The old man worked in the county treasurer's office. Times were tough. They came one night and picked him up for embezzlement. I was a sophomore in high school then. He hung himself in the cell while he was waiting trial. We were on relief until the old lady started drinking so heavy they had to put her away. The night they took her away, I had a mad on at the world. I took a car off the street and wrapped it around an oak tree. They gave me three years in reform school. When I got out I became a runner for a big book in Detroit. Now I've got the sort of a setup every jerk in the world thinks he'd like. And you know what?" He laughed, a flat dead sound in the room. "I still want to be an architect!"

She sipped her drink and looked over at me. Her eyes glowed. "Or take Cliff. He's like a little boy who has broken all of his favorite toys in a fit of spite. Now he's trying to show the world what a rough little kid he is."

"That's not quite fair, Melody."

My steak sandwich came in. Just the sight of it made my jaws ache. It was huge and good. But putting food in my stomach was not the cure for the shakiness inside me. The beating Gilman and De Rider had laid on wasn't something that would go away in a day. I thought of the fictional heroes of the hard-guy school, of the way they can bounce back from a pasting that should have put them in hospital beds. The human frame is a lot more delicate than such lead characters are permitted to show. I knew, testing my own weakness, that I would be less than right for at least four days, maybe a week.

In the back of my mind was the mirage of a big feather bed into which I could crawl. The door opened abruptly behind me and I turned, putting the last bit of the sandwich in my mouth. Larry Kreshak came in, the bandage glaring white against his bronzed forehead.

His anger was so great that it brought him ridiculously close to tears, giving his bright full lips a pouty look. He came toward me in slow gliding steps and he couldn't look at my face. He looked at the second button on the front of my shirt.

"Larry!" Tony said sharply.

I wiped my hands on the napkin and tossed it over onto the tray. "Let him get it out of his system, Tony." I said.

Larry planted his feet and stood in front of me, swaying almost imperceptibly. Tony was coming around the side of the desk.

"Go ahead, Larry," I said. "You're a rough boy. You and your brother. I think you can probably take me, but that's all you'll do. But I'm telling you this, and listen hard before you start anything. You touch me and sooner or later I'll kill you. You can wait for it and wonder how I'll do it."

It was pure bluff. But I knew that he'd seen the car plunging toward him and knew that he already had the taste of death on his mind. Tony saw what was happening and he stayed where he was, near the desk.

You could almost hear the wheels turning in Larry's mind. The big grille of the car, leaping toward him, had made a deep mark on his soul. The ripe lips still pouted and his fists were still clenched, but the ridged muscles of his arms softened and the cords in his size-eighteen throat became less evident.

He came apart all at once, the tears spilling out of his eyes and the sick sounds coming from his throat. The swaying became more evident and he turned blindly back to the open door, his shoulder thudding against the side of the doorframe as he blundered through.

Tony went over and closed the door. "Damn you, Bartells! You've spoiled him for me. They'll never be any damn good again, either of them. They'll be trying so hard to prove that they're still men that they'll go around looking for trouble. I can't have that here."

"You ought to be glad you found out he can be bluffed. It might have showed up when you really needed it, Tony. Now you can hire some real rough boys, instead of a couple of muscle-bound pansies."

Melody giggled thinly. We turned and stared at her. Tony cursed and went over to the shaker he had left on the table beside her chair. There was nothing in it but ice. She looked at us and giggled again. Her eyes weren't tracking.

"Should've ha san'wich," she said thickly.

"She was knocking them off as fast as she could fill the glass," he said. "Wouldn't you know."

"Give her a small break. Sometimes you'll grab the first anesthetic you can reach, Tony."

" 'Nesthetic," she mumbled. "S'right, Cliffy, Cliffy. 'Mere. Help Melly up. Gah walk 'round, Cliffy. Walk Melly 'round. S'hot in here. Too hot."

She struggled up out of the chair, reaching for me. Her eyes went wide and she looked through me and beyond me. There was a greenish tinge to her complexion. She grunted softly and I caught her just as she went as limp as a rag doll. She fell across my arm, her head lolling forward, the silver-gold hair spilling, her contorted posture straining the seams along the back of the black dress.

"Pick her up," Tony said with enormous weariness.

I got one arm under her knees and the other around her shoulders. Her head fell back as though her neck was broken, and I let her slide a little so that my right arm partially supported her head.

"Pull her dress down over her knees, Tony," I said.

I followed him down the hallway to a small bedroom. He pushed the buzzer, and a few moments after I had put her on the bed and straightened out her limp body, a sturdy maid in a starched uniform appeared. She didn't change expression as she saw the unconscious girl.

"Undress her and put her to bed, Clara. Make her as comfortable as you can. Lock her in and leave a note for her to buzz you when she feels well enough to leave."

"Yes, sir," Clara said stolidly. We left and she closed the door quickly.

"She's had about all she can take," I said. He nodded absently.

"Keep me up to date, baby," he said, and I left to call a cab from the desk.

11

I HAD THE CAB drive me slowly by the Coral Strand. The Chevvy was back on its wheels and I guessed that some of the crowd that gathered had made themselves useful. There were still about twenty people standing aimlessly around, gawking at the scene, plus a pack of kids. They were in two groups, one around the greasy landlady, who was still talking so animatedly that her jowls vibrated in the sunshine, the other around a self-appointed guide, who was pointing at the hedge.

The cab driver said, "Wonder what the excitement is there."

"Murder number three, maybe."

"Geez, don't say that. I got orders not to even talk about the first two with the fares. Funny how a guy changes. There I am hackin' in Philly and another hatchet killing is just something in the paper, like the weather.

Down here I get nervous. You'd think it was my head they been beatin' on."

"That's just public spirit."

"You think so? Maybe I'm beginning to like this crummy town, you mean. The wife had to come down to a hot climate, so here I am. Give me a rainy night in Philly with the fares beatin' on the hack windows any time. Here you are. Western Auto."

Saturday. A hot quarter after five. The office was closed. Letty had marked me. I didn't want to walk down the alley. The manager of the Western Auto, my landlord, came out and cut me off. He had a bleak look.

"Mr. Bartells, I want to tell you that I didn't like this morning's occurrence."

"No?"

"There were several customers in the store. It upset them."

"It upset me too, Mr. Rourke."

"Where is that person? Is there any danger of her trying again?"

"They've got her over in the women's ward at the county lockup. If they let her out, I'll tell her to try again after store hours."

"Mr. Bartells, I don't think this is a time for levity."

"You should have seen me giggling and scratching myself while that cannon was going off in my face."

He softened a little. "It must have been pretty frightening. I don't mean to be difficult about this, but . . ."

"All I can say is that I hope it doesn't happen again."

"That's very fair of you. You realize, of course, that I'll have to bill you for the splintered step?"

"Of course."

We bowed and beamed and backed away from each other like a pair of Japanese diplomats. He was a nice enough little guy, once you learned to overlook his tendency to take himself seriously.

As he reached the door of the store he called, "By the way, that little girl from your office was here twice. She told me to tell you she'll be back."

That was a new angle. Heretofore Kathy had avoided my apartment with all the determination and most of the grace of a *torero* staying clear of the horns, while still making it look to the public at large as though the horns were, in truth, exceedingly close to the embroidery. It had become a game of maneuver, with me outclassed from the start.

I climbed the steps and unlocked the door, too dulled with fatigue to give much of a damn. I told myself that even if I found Kathy asleep on my bed, I'd drop just inside the door.

I closed the door, stripped off my clothes, and took a shower. There was still a jail stink clinging to me. I scrubbed until I realized that it was the sort of odor that doesn't come off with a brush. It comes from inside.

It was no good trying to plan what to do about Trumbull. My mind wouldn't function. As a concession to Kathy I put on a pair of lurid pajamas before tumbling into the sack. I wondered vaguely when the heat would break. Sleep was a black sloping tunnel and I was sliding down it, head first, faster and faster. . . .

. . . Horace had a toy Cadillac a foot long in his hand and his face was all screwed up and he was crying the way a child cries as he hammered me over the head with it. I couldn't make him stop because I was holding a full stein of beer in each hand and there was no place to put them down and I couldn't spill any, or Letty would find out and tell Melody. Melody was above my head somewhere, calling to me. . . .

The dream split across the middle and blew away like smoke, and I was sitting up on the studio couch listening to a determined banging on my door, hearing Kathy calling, "Cliff! I know you're in there. Cliff!"

The world outside had the purply color that comes with the last of dusk, the first of night. I blundered up, reaching for my robe, smashing my toes against a chair leg, yelling, "O.K., O.K.!" I found the floor-lamp button and squinted my eyes against the brilliance.

I opened the door and found what she had been hammering with. She was just slipping the moccasin back onto her foot. She straightened up and looked with mock horror at what showed of the pajamas under the bottom edge of the robe. She laughed nervously. "I'm glad I found out about *that* in time."

"Come on in. Wait a minute while I wake up."

She walked in with every imitation of boldness. What spoiled the effect was the way she had gone back to her place after the office closed and changed from her office costume into a pair of copper-riveted ranch-type blue jeans and a light blue T shirt two sizes too large for her. She looked about thirteen, except where the jeans were the tightest. I wanted to laugh at her, and I wanted to kid her about the false sense of security a bunch of copper rivets were giving her, but I guessed that it was neither the time nor the place.

She sat down on my straight chair, her knees close together and her hands folded in her lap, as demure as the first day in junior high. I left the door open on a hunch and went back into my midget-sized bathroom, let the water run cold, caught it in my cupped hands, and scrubbed my face with it. Sleep was driven further back into my mind, but it was still there, with all the potential of a boulder balanced on a cliff edge. I ran a comb through my wet hair and went back out. I gave her a cigarette.

"Now, is this so bad? Door open and everything?"

She ignored me. "Please forgive the way I look, Cliff. I'm a fright, I know. But I was so afraid of missing you that I didn't want to go back and change again."

She leaned forward as I held the match for her cigarette. As she exhaled the first breath she leaned back in the chair, then sat bolt upright again, as though to lean back were an offer of weakness.

"That woman didn't hurt you, Cliff?"

"She missed me. It wasn't her fault. She hid behind the car. I was a damn fool not to think of that."

"By the time I found out about it they'd already taken you to jail. I tried to see you, Cliff, but they were horrible to me, and they told me that ridiculous story about maybe you killed that Franklin man. I told them it was a lot of stupid nonsense. Arthur had gone home and I got him on the phone. I went back to the office and used my key and called him from there. That little worm!"

"You expected Arthur to help me? Weren't you being a little naïve?"

"I guess I was. He coughed and mumbled and coughed, and I could almost hear him jigging and dancing away in his hall. Then I said to him that he better make up his mind fast whether he was going to help you or not, and he said that I ought to be able to see what his position was and they wouldn't listen to him anyway. I hung up on him. I don't even know if I'll have a job Monday morning."

"You will. That's a promise."

"Cliff, that isn't what I came to see you about. Just as I let myself out, I heard the phone start ringing. I unlocked the door again and it was that same man calling from Tampa. He said it was very important for you to call him and he'd wait for your call and I should try to find you and give you the message. I went back to my place and changed and then I went to the police station again. They still wouldn't let me see you. So I went and ate and came back and tried again. Nobody would tell me anything except that you'd left with that tall blonde girl. She *is* pretty, Cliff."

"Uh-huh."

"And I could tell by the way she looked at you at the hotel that she likes you. A lot. They say she's going to have an awful lot of money."

"Word gets around fast, doesn't it? Now that you've got it all set, how many children do you think she and I'll have?"

"I didn't mean that! I just said that she likes you."

"Didn't you get off the track?"

"I came back here to see if you'd come here with her and you hadn't and then I had to try to find out where she lived to see if you'd gone there. It took me a long time to find out that she's over in that awful little tourist trap. The one who told me was Bobby Gilman. As usual, he tried to date me. He acted funny, you know?"

"I've got a few plans that may have him acting even funnier."

"Don't, Cliff. He's really bad. He was two years ahead of me in high school here, you know, and I know what he's like. There was terrible trouble when he was in high school. He went to a dance place and cut a boy in the face with a broken bottle. If he hadn't been the best player on the football team, I think they might have done something to him. He and Nick De Rider are . . ."

"They had their fun with me today, kitten."

"Cliff! Did they hurt you?"

"Not badly. Go on with the history."

"I got out there just when the ambulance did. Those two sissy boys that work at the Kit-Kat were hurt. Somebody tried to tell me you ran over them on purpose with Mr. Lavery's car."

"I did."

"What! Cliff, what a dumb thing to do! Well . . . maybe you had a reason. Nobody had any idea where you'd gone. I came back here and waited for a long time, sitting on your steps, and then I got hot and thirsty and went down and had a root beer at Martin's and read a magazine and then came back, and Mr. Rourke was just leaving and he told me you were up here. I guess you didn't wake up until I started hitting the door with my shoe." She stood up. "Now that you've got the message, I better . . ."

"Honey, I'm so dead on my feet I'm harmless. Sit tight while I call my friend. Maybe I'll have an errand for you."

"But I . . ."

"Be domestic. Bourbon's on the second shelf on the left. Glasses over the sink. Ice in the tray."

I dialed the operator and gave her Johnny Alfrayda's number in Tampa. As I waited I could hear Kathy working the lever that loosens the ice cubes, hear her dropping them into the glasses.

"Hello?"

"Johnny? Cliff."

"It took you a hell of a long time. Look, boy, you know that item you wanted me to tell you about if I happen to see one?"

"How can I forget? But . . ."

"Leave off the buts for a couple minutes. Look, I found the item just like you want. And the guy is real anxious to sell. Let me think how I word this, Cliff. I'll just say that the retailer is a guy I can't vouch for because I've never done business with him before, but he had the right references."

"What! How would a guy like that get . . ."

"You sound like you know him, boy."

I wrapped my fingers around the cool glass Kathy handed me. "I think I do. But go ahead."

"He called me today at quarter after twelve and . . ."

"He what?"

"Cliff, boy, if you keep stopping me every two words, this is going to be one hell of a phone bill for you."

"I'm sorry. It just startled me. You see, I had a guy in mind, and I know for sure that my guy was in no position to call you at twelve-fifteen."

"So it was his partner. So now shut up, please. I'm

sure this merchandise is exactly what you're looking for, but that doesn't mean that his retailing ethics are going to be so good. He got the word that you are all right to deal with, but he says that he's very anxious to go out of business and leave this part of the country. It's for his health, I think. He told me he'll bring the merchandise there rather than you coming up here. He wants to know if Monday night will be all right."

"Monday night, as far as I know, will be O.K."

"Now look. You come over tonight. I want to talk to you about this purchase. I'll tell you the rest of what he said."

"I can't, Johnny. I can't do it. I'm too bushed. I've had a bad day."

I could almost see his shrug. "O.K., so tomorrow."

"Thanks, Johnny."

"The references were O. K., or I wouldn't do anything. You understand that."

"I understand it."

He hung up. I set the phone over on the table and sipped the drink. Kathy sat across from me on the straight chair.

"Strong enough, Cliff?"

"Huh? Fine, fine, Kathy. Yours looks a little weak."

"It is. It's plain water." She laughed nervously.

I scowled at her. "You're as edgy as a child bride. For heaven's sake, calm down. You're giving me the jitters."

"I better go, Cliff."

"Then *go.* Stop up again sometime. Carry a knife the next time you drop in. Your apprehension is flattering, but it gets tiresome." I bit each word off hard, knowing as I spoke that I was taking out on her a heavy anger that she had not caused.

She stood up as meekly as a punished child and said, "Good night, Cliff."

I let her walk alone to the open door and then remorse hit me. I got to the door and caught her gently by the shoulders just as she stepped out onto my landing.

I turned her around gently and she looked up at me through those long lashes, the same stunt she had pulled in the hotel grill.

"Kathy, I'm seven kinds of pig. I'm sorry. You've done me a good turn and that's no way to repay you."

I pulled her slowly in through the doorway and moved

her to one side so that her shoulders were against the
wall. She held both palms flat against my chest as though
ready to push me away as I kissed her. Her lips were
like warm marble under mine, still and motionless, hard.
She seemed to be holding her breath. The air had a hot
stillness. And then I heard the distant grumble of thunder, like a giant that stirred restless in the east.

A wind, wetly cool, brushed our faces. It strengthened
and, as the blue-white of lightning flickered distantly, the
gust strengthened, catching the open door beside us,
swinging and slamming it shut with pistol-shot violence.
A startled cry came from her and she took a half step to
the side. The room went dark and I knew that she had
inadvertently kicked the wall plug loose.

Then her lips came alive, moving under mine, and her
hands, flat against my chest, slowly curled, the stiff
fingers digging into me. I slid my hands down from the
firm shoulders to the tight slim waist, feeling the play
of muscles there as, with her shoulders still against the
wall, she thrust her hips forward.

We made blind, stumbling steps across the room, and
then she was on the couch beside me, facing me. She had
gone, in the space of seconds, beyond thought and beyond coherence, beyond plan, beyond everything except
a twisting, contorting, consuming violence, a vast un-
thinking impatience, a demand as clear as though it were
written in letters of fire across the room's shadows.

I rose with her on the wave crest of a thing long denied, only vaguely conscious of reaching between us and
thumbing open the buttons of the jeans, then sliding my
hand around her and peeling the jeans down over the
twin convexities of alive plum-tautness, dimly conscious
of the thud as the moccasin fell at the end of the couch,
of her breath that was like the beating of a wing against
my throat, of the infuriating intricacies of robe belt, of
the twin alivenesses hard under the blue T shirt, of the
whole urgent mounting need of her, as vivid as a scream.

And then the lightning made a long-sustained flash,
touching her face and the dark tangle of her hair. In that
moment that the lightning lasted I thought of how we
had been to each other, and of the office joking, and of
the game we had played, and how now, in a few moments, the heart would go out of that game and it would
no longer be a game, ever again, but something else in

which there would be a sadness, and she was a girl who would not let the sadness show, no matter how it hurt, no matter how far from her it placed that ever present dream of marriage.

And as the lightning ceased I fought against that voice in my mind that told me it was too late to stop. I rolled to the side and I thrust her away from me, thrust her so hard that she struck the wall and cried out.

I went into the bathroom and turned on the light and slammed the door and ran cold water in the sink. I thrust my face into it and then took a big towel and scrubbed my face hard. I pulled the belt to the robe tight, found a cigarette on the shelf, lit it, and sucked the smoke deep with a shuddering breath.

When I went back out she sat in the dark on the edge of the couch.

"Decent?" I asked. My voice sounded too loud.

"Yes."

I found the floor plug and worked it back into the socket. She sat on the edge of the couch, her arms resting on her knees, her hands hanging limp from the slim brown wrists. It seemed an oddly pathetic touch that she should be wearing one moccasin, the other at the foot of the couch resting on its side.

She raised her head and gave me a weak smile. Her lips were swollen and her eyes were heavy-lidded. I kicked the missing shoe over to her. "Here. Put it on."

She slipped her foot into it. "Now you know about me," she said hopelessly.

"What do I know?"

Her smile was crooked. "I can play a good defensive game in a car or even on the beach, but anything remotely resembling a bedroom and I'm licked." Her breath caught in a sob. "Hell, hell, hell, hell," she said tonelessly.

"Now I know why you were nervous," I said, trying to keep my tone light.

"I thought it would happen this way." She stood up. Her shoulders sagged. She yawned heavily, covering her mouth with her hand.

"No harm done," I said.

She nodded. "I know. You were the one who stopped. I couldn't have stopped. That's what I didn't want you to know about me. I guess I should be grateful or something. But I want to kick you and hit you with my fists. I want to yell bad words at you, Cliff. I suppose you stopped because of those scruples like Frenchmen have. You know. Bad form if the girl's a virgin."

"That isn't why I stopped. I didn't know you were."

"I am," she said dully. "And I'm twenty-three. Maybe they should give me a medal. If they do, I'll hand it over to you, Cliff."

"I stopped because I had the funny idea I'd be losing something instead of gaining something. Maybe you know what I mean. Maybe you don't."

We were at the door. She patted my cheek awkwardly. "I'll try to figure it out sometime. Anyway . . . thanks, I guess."

She jumped as the thunder came crashing on the heels of another bolt of lightning. The rain came, roaring in the distance, louder and louder, then smashing down all around.

"You can't go out in that."

"I think I better had, Cliff. I think it would be a good thing."

She went slowly down the steps. The rain was so heavy that it was like a curtain. By the time she reached the last step I could barely see her. And then she was gone.

I went into the kitchen and poured my glass half full of bourbon. She hadn't replaced the tray of cubes. They had shrunk away from the metal in the heat. I put three of them in the whisky and swirled the glass a few times. The next flash and crack of thunder had a wider gap between them. The storm was passing over.

I drank what was in the glass, the ice cubes hitting my teeth. I hadn't waited long enough. It was tepid. I gagged over the last swallow. There was barely time to get to bed before the numbness crept across my mouth. I lay naked in the darkness and the faint scent of her was on the pillow. I wondered if the day would ever come when I would understand myself, and know why I did things, or why I kept from doing other things. I tried to drown the wanting for Kathy by thinking of Melody. It didn't work, but it reminded me of unfinished business. I called Tony and asked him to tell her to phone me before she tried to leave. He was still annoyed with me. Then I slept.

12

Sunday morning I woke up shivering in a gray and frigid dawn, suffering from the false idea that I felt pretty good. Once I got on my feet I learned better. For some reason every tooth in my head felt loose in its socket. My joints felt aged and rusty and my head ached, not on the surface and not inside, but oddly about three feet behind me, every place I stood.

Kathy's cigarette butt, smudged with pink, was mashed in the ash tray near where she had sat. Beside the ash tray was the glass, with a faint pink smear at the rim, a half inch of stale melted ice in the bottom of it. The room felt as though the water should have frozen again.

I washed the body and husked it down with a towel until there was a faint glow. I scrubbed the green brass off my teeth. With the windows closed and the heater going, the place felt less like a tomb.

When the organism is at a low ebb, morale demands more care in adorning it. After the closest shave I could give myself, I broke a pair of new shorts out of a cellophane wrapper, added an imported shirt, British Daks in gray flannel, dark wool socks, cordovan loafers, and one of Bronzini's quieter ties, and topped it off with the old tan-brown Harris jacket, the hound's-tooth one. Keys, money, cigarettes, change, pocket knife. Anything else, Bartells? Come on, think.

You've got the jitters. You're trying to keep yourself from thinking this out. Where does Trumbull fit? Who killed Franklin? How can you tie Trumbull and Franklin and the obvious pros who have contacted Johnny up into one neat package, wrapped for delivery?

And who are you going to cross, Bartells? You know you're going to cross somebody. Maybe even just for the hell of it. Just to blow the lid off this pat little life, this neat little Florence City existence.

Problem one, Melody. I stood by the heater and nibbled on my knuckles and thought about Melody. The reasoning that seemed so clear yesterday was no longer so good. In the morning light the idea of Trumbull killing Melody seemed absurd. But Tony had bought it. He'd bought it strongly enough to protect me on the very clear assault charge that could have been brought in the affair of the murderous Cadillac.

I'm a neat housewife. I emptied the ash trays, washed the glasses, and made up the bed. It didn't help me think any more clearly.

Thankful that my pet diner is a twenty-four-hour deal, I walked over and had a Sunday breakfast. I was ahead of the church group. Juice, waffles, sausage, toast, and three cups of coffee.

Then I drove to the Kit-Kat. The gate was chained and there was no watchman. I parked my car outside the gate, picked a good spot, and went over the ornamental fence. The Cadillac was where I had left it, but with the top up to keep out the night dew. An early charter boat chugged down the bay, heading for the channel, heading out for the big ones. I looked over at the bridge I had just crossed as I walked across the parking area. Three fishermen stood motionless on the bridge, like stuffed dummies. Decoys.

Mist was clinging to the bay shore line, made by the cold air and the heat still in the ground and shallow water. Two cars rattled over the bridge plates. I knocked on the side door, waiting a long time, knocked harder. No answer.

I heard the scuff of gravel and turned. Melody came smiling toward me. I didn't really know how worried I had been about her until I saw her.

She had a fresh bright morning face. "Hello!"

"Hello to you!" We spoke in early-morning voices.

"The clothes," I said.

She looked ruefully down at the too-short skirt. The pink cashmere sweater was too tight, the tweed jacket that matched the skirt too small across her shoulders. "Awful, isn't it? I woke up about an hour ago. I found the note to call you, with a room key on top of it. I decided you'd be pretty savage at this hour. These clothes were in the closet, so I borrowed them. I sneaked out and found, after the outside door latched behind me, that the fence presents a problem. So I've been sitting by the pool pretending I own the place."

"Funny game for you. You could own a place like it now."

The breeze was crisp. She turned toward it, her hands jammed into the jacket pockets. I wanted her carved on the bow of my next clipper ship, but it would have to be a good guy to capture the way that silvery hair moved in the wind.

"Hungry, I suppose?"

"I had my eye on a sea gull, but he didn't come close enough."

"You know what I like?"

She moved closer. "What?"

"You're not wringing your hands and telling me how sorry you are you made such a horrid, nasty display of yourself yesterday afternoon."

"That was three other girls. Silly girls. Emotional types. Now, take me. I'm sound. I'm there. I'm with it."

"No more problems?"

"Problems, sure. But today is the day I could have been dead. But I'm not. So every moment is clear profit, Cliff. Thank you for today, and for all the rest of my days, every one."

"Then you're sold on that idea I had?"

"I keep thinking about Furny. Murderers are people in the tabloids, or in the movies. Never anybody you know. So I pretended that this was a movie I was watching. Silly, isn't it? And Furny is a character in that movie. Then I thought of this character and how he wants things, and how badly Furny can want things. He is nice-looking, you know, and poised and all that, not sinister in any way—except that wanting, and knowing that somehow he'll get what he wants. Looking at him that way, I can make myself believe that he wouldn't really let *anything* stop him. Whether or not he would stop at murder, Cliff, is something I don't know and you don't know. So I must tell myself that he wouldn't, and then I'm being smarter than if I went around saying that life is neither a movie nor a tabloid."

"I agree. You're sound. Now leave us leap gaily over the fence."

I walked her to the spot where I had crossed. I boosted her up to where she could stand with her feet on the crossbar, between the iron spikes. I had her bend over and hold onto two spikes for balance, then turn one foot around carefully, then the other, and, still holding the spikes for balance, jump down backward. She landed off balance, took three steps backward, and sat down hard, grunting with the impact, rolling back onto her shoulders so that for a second or two her slim legs bi-cycled in the air.

I dropped on the far side of the fence just in time to give her a hand up. Then, still holding hands, laughing though there was nothing to laugh at, we ran to my car and I took her back across the bridge into the city, took her back as though she were a prize that I had won through some feat of arms.

After breakfast in a diner we drove out to the Coral Strand and I parked beside the upright Chevvy. As she went inside to change into her own clothes I looked the car over. Most of the oil had run out and the left fend-ers and door were dented, but not badly. At the most a fifty-dollar repair bill.

I glanced down the line of doors just in time to see the landlady yank her head back in like a turtle retreat-ing into its shell.

Melody came out wearing a tailored suit in a fawn shade of soft flannel, with a blouse that was pale green, a froth of ruffles at her throat, a green barrette clamping her hair in an unsuccessful attempt at severity. The over-the-shoulder alligator bag was gleaming, enormous, and new.

The sun appeared for a little time and then retreated behind the overcast. On the way to Tampa I tried to explain Johnny Alfrayda to her, and explained why I would have to leave her at the hotel while I talked to Johnny.

She sat close to me, and she said, "But after you find out and come back and get me, you'll know about Furny, won't you?"

"I'll have some better ideas about Furny."

"Today I'm not me. This is all festive. I'm brand-new. Today I was never married, and I've never had an Aunt Elizabeth, and Furny is somebody in a Dick Tracy se-quence. I'll wait for you in the hotel and I'll pretend all kinds of things as I wait. Hurry back to me, Cliff."

"Rainey's still in town?"

"Yes. He's made arrangements for Aunt Elizabeth to be cremated. There was a letter he showed me where she said that was her wish. It sort of surprised me. It will be done Monday, and then he's taking the ashes back with him on the plane for burial in the family plot. When I get up there I'll make the arrangements for a memorial service for her in her church. He seemed to think that's the way to handle it."

"There are other things to be done, I suppose."

"He has the car to dispose of, and then there's all her personal effects that she brought down with her. I suppose the best thing to do with the clothes is give them to some local charity. I can go through her things with Letty and . . ."

"Letty isn't available."

"I forgot that. How awful! Can you take me to see her when we get back? Could you get her out, Cliff?"

"I can make a try at it. They'll have had one of the county psychiatrists look her over by now. If they want to be decent about it, they'll mark it off as shock, temporary insanity, and let her go. I won't press charges."

"When are you going to tell me how you were to blame for his being killed, Cliff?"

"Did I say I'd tell you?"

"No. But I'd like to think that you will tell me—sometime."

"I'll tell you now. I gave everybody a different figure on what I'd pay for the stones. When the figure came back to me it was the same one I'd told the Franklins. It could have been coincidence. I got Letty alone and convinced her Horace was working with the crooks. So she promised to keep her mouth shut, but instead she popped off to him, I guess. He got scared and contacted the ones who did the job. With murder hanging over their heads, they could risk a second one to be safer as far as the first one was concerned."

Her voice was odd as she said, "Then you gave me a different figure too. What would you have done if the amount you told me had been the one that—that came back to you?"

"I would have considered you as a possible bird dog."

"Bird dog?"

"One of those greedy little people who point out the big chance, then step aside to let the pros handle it."

I could feel the quick change of mood. All the unforced gaiety of the morning had left her.

"Can you ever take anyone on trust, Cliff? And don't try to tell me that was trust, that first night you took me out. Don't lie to me. That was a little act of yours, wasn't it?"

"Of course."

"I . . . don't think I like that."

"Suit yourself. I'm being honest with you now. Right now, in my mind. I've dealt you out of it. Not on faith. Not because for the first time in too long I've found a woman I can think of as a person and talk to as a person. No, honey. Because I've fed you the right words and you've reacted the right way. You're out of it. The lush blondes who can sucker the investigator are a movie cliché. Any investigator or ex-cop who has got beyond the diaper stage knows that the lusher they are, the more larceny they have in their hearts. You know why? Because pretty girls go through life with people bowing and scraping on all sides. They can't help thinking and believing they're very special people. And, as special people, the laws and rules don't apply. So please don't give me the trembling lip and the wide, wide hurt eyes, just because I didn't take you on faith from the first glance. That would have been something you could call pelvic reasoning. Feather-bed philosophy."

"Oh, you're a roughie, aren't you?" she said bitterly. "Skinned knuckles and a chip on your shoulder. Take a good close look at yourself sometime. You think you're being objective. Nuts! You're all twisted up inside. Women are your prize suspects just because they are women. I get so damn tired of this emotional double standard—this little-boy attitude that men are the only people in the world and women are some sort of annoying and interesting gadget. You make me sick."

She flounced over into the corner. When I glanced at her she was looking out her window at the flat country-side, at the desperately dull landscape of all parts of Florida more than a mile from the water.

"The little woman," I said. "Meet the wife. The brave little helpmeet standing shoulder to shoulder with her man. Mom. All men are little boys at heart."

"Now I have to run into an amateur Philip Wylie," she said acidly.

"I was just pointing out, friend, that an emotional double standard cuts both ways. You don't want to be a gadget for work and pleasure. And I don't want my head patted. I don't want to be the great American Dagwood, the fumble-puppy snuffling what's cooking on the stove, cute as a button."

"Nobody's trying to hog-tie you, Cliff."

"Nobody's going to," I said.

She turned and gave me a look of bright, almost lewd amusement. "Stick to gadgetry, son," she said.

"You can come back now."

She moved closer than before, so that the long line of flank pressed warm against me. She put her arm inside mine so that her fingertips rested on the inside of my wrist. She leaned her head back. "Tell me about my walk again."

"The exciting walk? That long-legged lilt? It's only exciting because it's a funny mixture. Enormous restraint and a promise of abandon. From the waist up you're carrying a candle down the center aisle. From the waist down you're Salome working loose from that last veil. It's schizophrenic."

"That's me. Split personality. Shall I tell you about my affair?"

"Sure."

"In '45. Two years after Dave was killed. Boy, was I sly! I worked on the guy for about a month. I thought he was shy. He came into the bookstore. Very distinguished Boston type. Taught mathematics at M.I.T. We dated a few times. I moved from my room to a little apartment, setting the stage. Came the evening. A dinner cooked with my own little hands. Wine. Candles. Perfume. Even a white birch fire in the grate. He brought flowers and another, mysterious package he didn't give me. I guess the lady had made herself too obvious—a very fatal flaw. Everything went quite swimmingly, as we old courtesans say, until I found out that he had his pajamas, a toothbrush, and a bottle of Alka-Seltzer in the package. It was too, too typically professional. And I remembered that he had told me once that he'd been an eagle scout. I was an utter failure. I got the giggles and I couldn't stop. He left in a great huff and he never came in to buy any more books. After he stalked out with his little bundle I locked the doors, drank all the rest of the wine, and laughed myself to sleep. End of romance. So I decided right then that I wasn't the cold-blooded type."

I was still grinning as we drove into Tampa. I dropped her at the hotel and told her to wait in the lobby. I went out to see Johnny.

He was alone at the big table in the dining room, a

baronial hall with a dark beamed ceiling. The Sunday papers were a litter around him. His man brought me some coffee.

Johnny sighed. "Read the papers. The country full of punks. Crazy kids running in wolf packs, beating up people. A hell of a thing."

I sipped the coffee. "Take a bow, Johnny. Those kids have read the papers too. They know that people like you have been making monkeys of the law ever since the old prohibition days. Every ratty little punk wants to be a big brave hood. People like you made a joke of the law for too long, and now it's beginning to show. They all want to be such big shots they can buy Hollywood houses and stock the bedrooms with actresses. So they start by beating the bejesus out of anybody who walks around alone at night."

He stared at me. "I'm retired. Besides, if I didn't like you, you woulda just got a bust in the chops."

I grinned. "Same approach the kids use, Johnny. You take it from me because you know where I stand. If this was my town and I was still a working cop, I'd try to make sure you'd really retire."

"Cops like you were, Cliff, always give us a headache. You square johns don't figure. Where you going to get your reward? Heaven? I'm glad most guys will settle for a little scratch."

I sipped the very good coffee. "Now you're winning my argument for me. That scratch you hand out, that grease applied in the right places—it's taken the guts and heart out of too many police departments. So now when they've got the wolf packs to deal with, they haven't got good cops to put out on beats in the bad neighborhoods."

His voice went silky. "But right now, Cliff, you're working with me, eh?"

"I'm a practical guy."

"You shouldn't talk to me that way, Cliff."

I actually think his feelings were hurt. He wanted so badly to think of himself as a retired businessman.

"Let's get to it. You said the fellow on the phone had references?"

"That's right. He mentioned names. He knew the right boys to unload on in other neighborhoods. Statz in K.C. Boly in Wilmington. I told him knowing the names maybe wasn't enough, so he told me he knew a red-haired guy who pulled the Rorson job in Scarsdale. The color of the hair is more than the law knows, so that was good enough for me. Those jewel boys, they got a hell of a grapevine. I told him maybe the cut had to be higher because this one was sour. He said O.K. and he said he knew it was sour, and so what."

"He wants it for Monday night in Florence City?"

"Yes, and he's got it figured out pretty good. I asked for the proof and last night a little kid brought this around." He pushed the wad of tissue paper across the table. I opened it. A small gold locket that had had a stone set in the front of it. The stone was gone. There were initials on the back of the locket, E.F.S. in fancy script. Elizabeth F. Stegman.

"Will he just hand it over?"

"Are you crazy, Cliff? He's no dummy, the way he talks. He knows how sour this is with the old lady dead and with that chauffeur dead, and he's not trusting anybody. It goes like this: At nine o'clock sharp you got to make the turn off the main road four miles south of Florence City onto Route Eight-o-eight. You know the place?"

"Yes. A gravel road with no traffic."

"You're to go no faster than ten miles an hour. Hold it right on ten and put a cross of black tar tape on your right headlight. Be alone and have the dough on the seat beside you. Make sure the door is unlocked, and the right window down. When you see two blinks from a flashlight on the shoulder, slow down to five miles an hour. As soon as a package is tossed in the window, stop the car. He said that's important. Stop dead. Don't turn off the lights or the motor. He'll give you a chance to check the package that's thrown in. A quick check. He says it'll all be there. Then toss the dough out. You know the way he wants the money. Old stuff, nothing bigger than a hundred or smaller than a twénty. Have the dough wrapped in a white package. Throw it about fifteen feet through the window. But don't start up. He'll shine the flashlight in at you when it's time to start up. When you do start, barrel on out of there. Make time. Go down to the end of Eight-o-eight and turn right. That road will bring you out onto the main highway. From then on you can do whatever you want to, so long as you don't retrace the route. Like it?"

"It sure puts him in the driver's seat, Johnny. I'll make a nice target sitting there."

"You want to make money, you got to take risks."

"He picked himself a spot. There's big groves there, and roads through the groves. Then there's bay front, and he could have a boat waiting. It looks to me as though he did a nice job of casing the area."

"He sounded smart, Cliff. He doesn't want to be crossed. Twice he cuts off and I get the rest of the call from another pay booth."

I met his eyes and then looked down at my coffee. The way things were beginning to shape up, I saw no point in telling Johnny that the actual payoff would be the three hundred rather than the four hundred the stranger had asked for. But Johnny had been in business a long time, and in his business a man either develops a batch of extra senses or he gets dead.

"I wouldn't like it much, Cliff, if you get fancy ideas," he said, very gently, as though chiding a rebellious child.

I looked over at his hand. The wrist was as heavily furred as an animal's. The square heavy nails were clean and shining. The hair on the third finger curled around the edges of the wide gold wedding band, worn for the wife who had died bearing the fifth child.

"You're going to bring the kids up down here, Johnny."

"You changing the subject?"

I met his glance. "I can hear the bells ringing in the back of your mind, Johnny. Like at a railroad crossing. You thought I was all right. Now you don't know. Now you're worried."

"I'm worried."

I put my elbows on the table and leaned toward him. "You were reading the paper this morning. Suppose it turns out really fancy around here, Johnny. Suppose it turns out like that guy in the temple after his hair grew back. Suppose the whole works comes falling down. Florence City is only a hundred miles away, Johnny. When kids get a little older they cover a lot of territory. You know that."

It was getting to him a little. He said, "That fella that pushed the temple down, Cliff. It fell on him, didn't it?"

"He wasn't fast on his feet."

He sighed. "O.K., Cliff. But look. I don't know a thing.

Go away now. You didn't say anything. If you did, I wasn't listening. He calls me back and I tell him it's all set."

I stood up, wiped my lips on the napkin, and tossed it beside the empty cup. "You're all right, Johnny."

He flushed angrily. "I'm getting old and soft in the head. It comes from being retired, maybe."

"You'll like it, I think."

He didn't answer me. The man let me out and I drove back to the hotel. The day was still overcast. Melody was waiting.

13

It was Sunday and there was no hurry. Melody got into the car beside me, and before we started up we shook hands solemnly and swore that until we got back to Florence City there would not be one single word about this thing that had brought us together.

We took the long way back. We drove across the Davis Causeway to Clearwater, going slowly, so that it was nearly noon before we arrived on Clearwater Beach. I found a place where we could rent suits, and the February day was so bleak that only the die-hards among the damyankee group were brave enough for the beach. The gray gulf waves looked surly as they came in. I was in first and I turned around and laughed at her as she stood in water up to midthigh, her shoulders hunched, her teeth chattering, gasping as the waves splashed up the front of the rented suit.

Afterward we ran on the beach until we were dry and relatively warm. We got dressed and found a small semicircular booth in the bar of a jukeless restaurant. We drank and looked at the people and felt that warm lethargy that comes after a lot of sea and sand and wind. We played the snide game of picking out people and deciding which animal they most resembled. A woman came in who was such a perfect bloodhound that Melody nearly strangled on her cocktail and I slapped her on the back.

The steaks were huge and tender.

Over coffee she said, "I have *so* much fun with you, Cliff."

"I'm an amiable type."

"But you're not. You're several different people. I like this one best."

I looked at her odd mouth, the square look of the lips, the threat of harshness, the hint of vulnerability.

"Here's my big chance," I said. "I've got you softened up. Now I should nail you down. How many guys get a hack at an heiress?"

She looked at me and her lips were parted an eighth of an inch and her breasts lifted under the green blouse and the tailored jacket with the new shallowness of her breathing. "How many guys?" she whispered. "Only one, Cliff. Only one. And the lady is all nailed down. Snap your fingers and hold out the hoop."

In that light her eyes were more blue than gray. I looked into them and saw the slow dilation of the pupils. The lids came down a bit over her eyes as though she were suddenly very sleepy.

"I'm holding out the hoop."

"Take me someplace and kiss me, Cliff, before I upset all these nice tourists."

We drove back to Tampa in the gray afternoon, slowly across the causeway, her head on my shoulder. One of the little places where there are picnic tables was empty and more secluded from the road than others. As I parked she turned in the seat so that her back was toward me. She pulled her long legs up and lay back into my arms, her face upturned, the lips still parted, her left hand creeping up to the nape of my neck and then tugging in a small and insistent way. As I kissed her she made a small comforted sound and moved more closely against me. There were no awkwardnesses and no fumbling. The long lines that were made to be traced by a slow sweep of hand were a warmness that had awaited that hand. The chaliced breast had a need that could be answered by the instincts of the hand, functioning without thought.

And then the horn blared as her shoulder rested against the horn ring. We jumped and her laughter was warm against my face. Sleepy contented laughter.

"It comes true this way, Cliff. After the no-good years."

"After all the no-good years."

"I didn't care before. Now I'll have Rainey break that codicil to the will. Those far-off names didn't mean anything when Aunt Elizabeth spoke of them. They didn't mean anything if they were going to be shared with Furny. Now they mean something, darling. Hawaii, Bombay, Cairo. All with you. All the beaches, all the drinks, all the funny places and doors we can lock behind us."

"We'll have to make two trips. The second time we'll look at the scenery."

"Now you can stop all this insurance nonsense, Cliff."

I looked down into her eyes. I looked for the gleam that would show she was joking. I looked for the lift at the corners of her soft mouth. She was solemn.

I laughed. "Let's not go too fast."

She pulled herself up, moved over on the seat. "Now see here, Cliff!"

"See here yourself, angel. Kissing me doesn't hang any sandwich sign on me reading, 'Property of Melody Chance.' I have things to do. After they're done we'll talk about plans."

"You're being dull."

"Then it's a characteristic and something you'll have to get used to."

"You're not telling me what I'm going to get used to."

There we were, snapping at each other. And suddenly we both had to smile. We told each other that we were being silly, so sorry, darling. We kissed again, but it was not quite the same. Neither of us was going to be dominated, and yet we both had the instinct to dominate.

It was funny that right in the middle of that second kiss I realized exactly how I was going to do the other thing. It was like some buried part of my mind had been nibbling at the problem, and all of a sudden the answer was there.

She felt the detached urgency in me.

She ran her fingertips down my cheek. "What is it? What have you just thought of?"

"Ways and means, honey. Too complicated to explain. I've got a phone call to make in Tampa."

She sighed and gave me a look that promised me that she would soon develop ways and means of making me forget any part of existence that was not all bound up with her. It made me remember, curiously, the way the female black widow tops off the mating act by devouring Mr. Spider.

We didn't talk and I wasted no time getting back to

Tampa. I left her in the car and went to a drugstore and got change for the phone. Anywhere in the country you can do it. Anywhere there's a phone. Just put a coin in, dial the operator, and say, "Get me the F.B.I." There is never any fuss about it. The nearest regional office pays the charge, even if you are pure crackpot and the nearest regional office is two hundred miles away. Outside of office hours the calls are fed to an agent who, according to the duty roster, is stuck with staying near a phone.

The voice was crisp and neat. "Federal Bureau of Investigation."

"My name is Clifford Bartells. I'm in charge of adjustments at the Florence City office of Security Theft and Accident. If you people are willing to take a fling at what might turn into a wild-goose chase, I'd like a conversation with you."

"Will the matter in question come within our jurisdiction, or is it a purely local problem?"

"Don't you co-ordinate with the Treasury on certain tax-evasion problems?"

"Where are you now?"

I told him and added that I had a car with me, but also a passenger who wasn't in on the situation. It was close to four o'clock. He told me he wanted to call me back in a few moments. I waited. When the booth phone rang I picked it up.

He said that I should come to a certain office in Tampa and be there at five. The passenger was my problem.

Yes, the passenger was my problem. I went out and put it up to her. I told her she could take the car and go back to Florence City, but that I would rather she wouldn't. We settled on a movie for her. A new musical, a leg show. I bought her a ticket and told her where to go when she got out.

And then I went to the office building. I went there with an empty feeling in my middle, because I knew that if they weren't buying, they could put me in a sad and awkward spot. I wanted them to buy. The office building was locked. A young man with dark red hair and a sunburned nose was standing inside the door waiting. He let me in and we walked back to the elevator.

"Turned cold," he said as he shut the door.

"The hot spell lasted a long time."

"It sure did," he said. He opened the doors and we walked down a corridor to an office door that was open.

Two other men were waiting. The older one of the two sat on a secretarial desk, a cigarette in the corner of his mouth. He looked like an advertisement for vacation living. The other one stood near him, a gaunt man with one of those smiles that turn down at the corners.

"We'll talk in there," the older man said, sliding off the desk. We went into the inner office and the door was closed on the inside by the redhead. They sat me close to the desk. The older man sat behind it. The other two remained standing. The older man lifted a small mike out of the desk drawer and set it in the middle of the desk. "No secrets here, Mr. Bartells. This is being recorded. Now, to save us a little time, I'll tell you that I've had a few minutes to look over our local records. We know you and we know your records. We assume this call of yours is connected with the Stegman murder and robbery. Now go ahead."

They listened without expression as I laid it on the line. I gave them every part of it. Then I told them what I expected and where I thought they might fit.

When I finished the man behind the desk said, "Please step out into the outer office for a few moments, Bartells. We'll call you."

I went out there and stood by a window, smoking, looking down into the street. Once in a while I could hear the deep tones of their voices.

The redhead opened the door. "Would you mind coming back in, please?"

I sat down and they let the silence mount.

"If we play along, and if your hunch is right, there isn't going to be any question in anybody's mind as to who set it up, you know."

"I know."

"You'll be up the proverbial creek. We can't be asked to protect you."

"All I ask is that you handle it in such a way that there'll be no tip-off before it happens."

"We're always curious about motivation, Bartells."

I shrugged. "Just say they hurt my feelings."

"We have a plan that ought to work. All you have to do is get the money from the bank no earlier than two o'clock tomorrow afternoon."

"You wouldn't want to tell me . . ."

"No, we wouldn't," the gaunt man said, speaking for the first time. "It'll be better if you just forgot you came here. We'll handle our end of it in such a way that no more than two men in the bank will know or guess, and they'll be in no position to talk."

The gray-haired man gave me a nod of dismissal. I went to the door with the redhead. As he opened it, the gray-haired man said, "Oh, Bartells."

I turned. "Yes?"

"Thanks."

"Don't mention it."

As we went down in the elevator, the redhead said, "Probably the cold spell won't last long."

"Not more than a few days."

"Always happens when the wind's in the north."

"At this time of year."

He opened the street door for me and said soberly, "You're right. Just at this time of year."

I went to the theater and bought myself a ticket and stood in the back until my eyes were able to function in the darkness. Halfway down the aisle I saw the gleam of her hair. There was an empty seat just beyond her. I mumbled an apology to the people on her right and they stood up to let me pass. Melody stood up too, her eyes on the screen. I edged by her and sat down and I could see that she hadn't noticed or recognized me.

I reached over and took her hand. She gave a little gasp and yanked it away. Then she whispered, "You darn fool!" She put her hand back where it belonged.

We watched chorus girls cavort.

At last I said, "Let's go."

I turned on the headlights as we drove out of the city. She had bought popcorn as we left the lobby. When we had to wait for a light, I pulled her closer and kissed her. Her lips tasted of butter and salt and her hair smelled of salt air and the sea.

She rode beside me in silence all the way back to Florence City. It was only as I slowed in front of the dark Western Auto and swung into the alley, the headlights sweeping the cinder-block wall, that she sat up on the edge of the seat.

I parked the car and we sat in the darkness. The neon sign atop the next building flicked on and off, on and off.

I ran my hand along the top of her shining head and then down to the back of her neck where the hair hung silky-thick. I squeezed it and it sprang back, alive, as I opened my hand. On the way up the steps she walked ahead of me and then stood quietly on the landing as I found the right key and opened the door.

I pushed the draperies back so that the neon sent its pale redness into the room, off and on, off and on, the furniture bulking oddly large in the intermittent shadow. It was a strange half hypnosis that had caught us, making words impossible, making motions slow, lethargic, tantalizing.

She linked her hands at the back of my neck and brushed her lips slowly back and forth across mine. When I tried to hold her tightly she pushed me away. I sat on the edge of the studio couch and watched her. She and the straight chair were between me and the widest window, between me and the red neon.

Her motions were slow, and as highly stylized as a dance. The one-second glow of the light and then the half second of darkness gave it the flavor and effect of one of those early films. She hung the suit jacket over the back of the chair, the fabric softening the hard outline of the wood. She looked down at her two hands close together at her left side, and I heard the thin sharp teeth of the zipper. She stepped out of the skirt and put it across the seat of the chair. She pulled the blouse up over her head and laid it over the back of the chair, over the jacket.

She turned in silhouetted profile to me, her heavy hair hanging forward as she reached both hands up behind her to the small of her back. The bit of fabric slid down her arms, held forward, and she turned and put it on the chair. It was like the dances of Java, where every motion must be done in exactly the proper way.

She sat on the chair then, and I heard the fabric whisper as she stripped the nylon hose down off her long legs. She stood up again, in profile, sliding other diaphanous fabric down the lean lovely line of legs, bending over, her knee lifting as she stepped out, putting the last bit of fabric on the chair.

And then she turned toward me and stood very still while the red neon in the distance went on and off a dozen times, silhouetting her with her lyre-curve of hip, as lovely as the stylized figure in a frieze. Then, each time the light came on, she was a half step closer to me, coming toward me with an almost unbearable slowness, coming like the sound of distant trumpets, dissonantly sweet like a song from brazen throats, a song of brass.

And it was a slowness, a soft and sliding slowness, a drowsy low-swinging slowness, tempering haste, fitted to sweet cadence, a merged and welded slowness that, when at last it could be borne no longer, climbed up a thousand microtonal scales, climbed into a joined quickness, a thick-twisting harsh unbearable quickness, blood cousin to pain, daughter of furies, a wild shout thrown upward at the stars in crescendoed apex, then sweet-fading back down through the endless spirals back to slownesses, and lingerings, and severances.

I gave her one of the two lighted cigarettes and watched the pink glow against her nose and cheeks as she inhaled. She sighed. Then with a voice as rusty as though it were the first time she had ever spoken, she said, "I love you."

"I love you. The last thing we were going to say, isn't it? We old sophisticates."

"Tell me I'm good."

"That's a funny request. You're good. You're the girl. The one. The dear. The cupcake. Why ask?"

"Vanity. I was never any good before. All elbows or something. Room left in my mind to stand off and watch. No room this time, Cliff. No room at all. Not with you. Now I ought to be ashamed. I ought to be ashamed for being easy, a pushover, a round-heeled wench. I'm trying to be ashamed. I'm really trying."

"How's it going?"

"Not well. I feel too good. Like a damnable cat on the hearth. Or more like I'd been washed down a river and over a dam and out to sea and now I'm floating out there, all drowned. Give me time. In a little while I'll be ashamed. I won't be able to look at you in the daylight. I'll blush and drop my eyes and stand all pigeon-toed."

"Simpering, maybe?"

"Probably. As long as we're on the topic of me, I will add that I am suddenly famished, starved, raving-mad hungry."

A half hour later, with the draperies pulled across the windows, the lights on, she sat at the table wearing my beach robe. As I put the scrambled eggs in front of her, she leaned her cheek against my arm. I took my plate and sat opposite her.

"You *are* blushing!" I said.

"Shut up, Bartells. Eat your eggs and don't look at me."

It was that sort of Sunday. The sort that starts you wondering why a man could have been so wrong so long.

14

WHEN I CAME OUT of the bathroom I found that she had folded the studio couch back into its normal width, and had neatly put the cover on it. It was a clear cold bright day. She looked composed, her face made up, her hair pulled back to such shining tautness that it gave a faintly Oriental tilt to her eyes. It was far, far easier to believe that she had just come in the door than to try to remember that she was Melody, who reached up for you out of the silken darkness of sleep.

Her suit looked as though it had just come from the cleaners.

"Hello, darling," she said.

"Do I detect a crispness of tone, my love?"

She sat in the straight chair, her legs crossed, her left hand on her hip, her right hand with the cigarette held off by her right shoulder, the elbow sharply bent. She looked as though she were waiting for tea to be brought.

"There are things we have to say, Cliff."

I picked a tie from the closet, stood in front of the bureau, and knotted it, seeing her reflection in the glass. "Speak out."

"In most ways," she said in a lecturer's tone, "we are right for each other. But there *is* a streak of antagonism."

"Before breakfast?"

"Please don't joke, Cliff," she said. "Last night, after one of . . ." She met my eye in the mirror and flushed. "Don't look at me like that. Last night we said a lot of things. Marriage was included."

She looked cute sitting there trying to be practical. "I think," I said, "that we decided it was inevitable, so we'd better relax and enjoy it."

She rose with one long graceful motion and came up behind me and put her hands lightly on my shoulders, leaned her forehead between my shoulder blades. "Now you can't watch me. Listen, Cliff. That was last night. This is today. This morning. You know, cold morning light. I want to forget that we said anything about marriage. You can think it over. There's no obligation at all. Then later one day you can ask me, if you still want to."

I turned around and lifted her chin with my knuckles. Her eyes were wet.

"You want a chance to reconsider, kitten?"

"No, you big darn fool! I don't want to trap you, is all."

"All right. I'll wait a few days. Now let me tell you something, Melody. Things can get very, very rough for me today or tomorrow or the next day. I'm going to be mixed up in a bad way with some people who might get very upset."

Her face went pale. "Cliff, I . . ."

"Don't talk. Listen. This isn't melodrama. Maybe I could have run out, with you. That might have been an answer. But I don't think it would have been a good answer. I think I may have gone broody on you, thinking of things left undone. This is my baby, and I'm not telling you anything about it except that I may not be a hell of a good insurance risk this week. I'm going to feed you breakfast and then I'm going to check you into the Coast Hotel. Until the all-clear sounds, you're going to stay in that room, have your meals served there."

I opened the bottom bureau drawer, reached under the shirts, and took out the small automatic, a Belgian .32, Browning patent. I checked the clip, jacked a round into the chamber, and put the safety in off position.

"Handle gingerly," I said. "Put it in your purse. If you want to fire it, you . . ."

She took it out of my hand, pushed the release that dropped the clip, worked the slide and ejected the round, thumbed the round into the top of the clip, and slapped it smartly back into place. "If I need it, I know how to work the slide."

"You fascinate me."

"Dave taught me about guns. He was a bug. I'm a good shot with rifle, pistol, revolver, and shotgun. But, Cliff, I think you're being an alarmist about . . ."

"Maybe so. Trumbull doesn't fit neatly anywhere as yet. So we'll make like boy scouts." She watched me as I put on the shoulder holster of soft, hand-tooled Mexican leather, socketed the .38 special into the spring clip. I put on the coat that was cut full enough to almost hide the bulge it made. A special is too big a gun for such a rig, but with the sole exception of the magnum, it's the only small hand weapon worth a hoot in a whirlwind for outdoor work.

Even her lips were pale. "Couldn't you tell me?"

"I'd rather not."

She shrugged hopelessly. I bought her breakfast at the diner, drove her to the Coral Strand, and waited while she got her bags and paid off the harridan, then followed the battered but serviceable Chevvy to a gas station for oil, then to the hotel parking lot. I carried her bags in and turned them over to a bellhop. I went upstairs with her and told her again not to leave the room. Back in the lobby I bought a few magazines and sent them up to her.

Then I went to the office. Wilma Booton gave me her welcoming sneer.

"Is anybody in there with Arthur?" I asked, pointing at the closed door.

"Mr. Myers is in conference."

I smiled at her and walked to the closed door. She wailed at me. I turned the knob and looked in. Arthur was dictating to Kathy. His feet, under the desk, were making little prancing sounds.

"Thanks, Arthur, for going to bat for me the other day."

He bounced up and down in the chair and his plump cheeks shook. "Now, Cliff! You know I couldn't have done you any good. The home office was on the phone this morning already. They say that they want a report on how we're . . ."

"Take a walk, Kathy," I said. She gave me a sullen look and went out. She slammed the door so hard that the big window rattled in its frame.

"Now what's eating her?" Arthur asked in an abused tone.

I sat in the chair Kathy had vacated. "Today, Arthur, is B day. Bonus day. Tonight we make the transaction."

His fat white fingers danced up and down the edge of the desk. "Are you sure? Are you positive? This is a terrible risk. All that money! We've got to be certain that this isn't somebody trying to cash in on . . ."

I shut him up by tossing the gold locket on the desk. He made little cooing sounds in his throat as he picked it up and examined it. "The inventory came airmail," he said, "and this was on it, with a big two-carat diamond in it listed at four thousand. You got the right people."

"Then suppose you get on the phone and get the bank. They've had time to accumulate the right kind of money. Tell them that I'll pick it up at their closing time, two o'clock. You'll have to be along, you know."

He reached for the phone. "I know, I know."

I stood up. "If you want anything, I'll be in my office for a little while."

He waved at me and I opened the door and went out, shutting it behind me. As soon as I was seated at my desk Kathy came in. She stood and stared at me, without friendliness. The difference was there, and it was startlingly obvious. Kathy the maiden was no longer. Her eyes were hard.

"Cliff, I wanted to tell you that you're the . . ."

She broke off quickly as Andrew Hope Maybree came in. His glasses sparkled like diamonds. He stood beside Kathy and put an arm possessively around her waist.

"Cliff, old man, I guess you should be one of the first to know. Kathy and I are going to be married."

"When was this decided?" I asked blankly.

He blushed. "Why, yesterday, Cliff. Yesterday. Happened like lightning."

Kathy's eyes were hard over her forced smile. The pattern wasn't hard to see. Andrew had been available to put out the fire. I looked at his salesman's face and at those big squirrel teeth, and the eyes shifty behind the sparkling glass, and I was surprised at the sudden enormous dislike I felt for him. Up until that moment I had tolerated him. Now the idea of him and Kathy made me feel slightly ill.

I came around the desk fast, shutting the office door. I thrust my face toward Andrew's, wearing a wide and delighted smile. "Why, that's wonderful!" I said. He coughed nervously and pulled his face away.

"Thanks, thanks, Cliff. I thought you might be . . ."

"Sore? Me? Hell, I'm delighted. It couldn't have happened to a nicer guy."

Kathy seemed relieved when his arm dropped from around her, as though she had been holding herself tense within his embrace.

Andrew licked his lips with a pointed tongue and giggled nervously. He couldn't seem to puzzle out my reaction.

I pumped his hand, grinding down on the knuckles until I saw him go a little white around the lips, and then I let go of his hand and thumped him on the shoulder, yelling, "You sly old dog, you!"

"Heh, heh, heh!" he laughed flatly, backing a bit away from me.

I slapped down on his shoulder with my left hand, and made a gentle-looking chop at his jaw with my right fist. It glazed his eyes for a fraction of a second and I felt his knees sag. I gave him a roar of laughter and another tap. He moved away fast, yanking out a handkerchief and holding it to the corner of his mouth, his eyes wide and alarmed. "Now look!"

I thumped his shoulder again. "Lucky dog, you!" I knuckled him in the middle and he wheezed hard, bending over a little.

Suddenly I was disgusted with myself and with what I was doing. It smacked of the probable reaction of Gilman or De Rider. I let my arm drop to my sides. It was then that Kathy charged around me. She was a small dark fury. She hammered him on the chest with both fists and kicked his shins with all her might, screaming, "I *hate* you! I *hate* you!"

"Kathy, honey, I . . ." He was trying to hold her off.

"I wouldn't marry you if you were the last man on earth!"

She turned away from him and plunged blindly for the door. Arthur swung it open and she ricocheted off him. He turned and stared after her. "Isn't she *peculiar* today?"

Maybree pulled himself together. He walked toward me with a quite unexpected dignity. "I don't know quite how you did that, Bartells. However you did it, it was a stinking trick."

It was probably his Sunday punch. I had plenty of time to decide to block it, and then change my mind and decide it would be better for my soul if I took it. His fist was like a sack of pebbles. It hit me on the corner of the jaw just in front of my left ear. Lights flared behind my eyes and my ears hummed. I shook my head and saw Andrew stalk out, holding himself very erect.

"Has everybody gone nuts this morning?" Arthur cried, hopping from one foot to the other.

I brushed by him and headed out, saying back over my shoulder, "I'll see you at the bank at five minutes of two, Arthur."

Commissioner Guilfarr looked at me across his desk. Sitting down, he looked like a man of more than normal height. Heavy raw shoulders and a wide chest, lean when seen in profile. His skull was long and narrow, with a prow of a jaw and a descending hook of a nose. Cropped reddish-gray hair, eyes as green as a cat's, a politician's mellow, flexible voice. Given a shade more intelligence and a new pair of legs instead of the stumpy little bandy legs that were almost a deformity, and he would most probably have been a state figure if not a national one. The knowledge of this was in him, and the hunger for unattainable places, and so there was a self-scorn in him that made everyone uncomfortable.

"Chief Powy will be right over," he said. "Surely there's nothing *you* could tell so important that we have to wait for Powy."

"I guess you'll have to humor my little whim," I said.

His mouth twisted as though he had tasted something unpleasant. Powy rapped at the door and came in without waiting for an invitation. The little eyes swept across me and the bullfrog voice said, "Any business Bartells has with the law ought to be taken up with me before—"

"Shut up and sit down, Powy," Guilfarr said wearily.

Powy shoved a walnut chair closer to the desk with his foot and eased himself tenderly into it.

"Now if you can bring yourself to talk, Bartells . . ." Guilfarr said.

I had to make my act good. I gave Powy a fawning smile. "The Chief and I understand each other, Commissioner. I admit I was pretty stubborn for a while. But now I understand that the best thing I can do is co-operate, all down the line."

Powy coughed and stared at me.

I said quickly, "I know that Chief Powy is going to get

word the moment that we make the withdrawal from the bank. I want it to be clearly understood that I'm not bucking the department. I held a grudge for a time and I admit it."

Powy chuckled. "So the boys beat a little sense into you, eh?"

I made my smile as rueful as I could. "I don't want any more of that. No, sir!"

"Am I to understand," Guilfarr said, "that you've made contact with the murderer?"

"That's right. I'm to hand over the money tonight. I've been thinking it over. I'm over a barrel either way. But I'd rather be on the side of the law."

Powy leaned forward in his chair. "When and where?"

"Now, wait a minute. I'm going to be the man on the spot," I said. "I'm willing to cross them up, but I don't want it handled in such a clumsy way that I'm going to end up with holes in me. I'll tell you on one condition."

"You're not in any position to make conditions after what you've just said," Guilfarr advised gently.

"It's a reasonable condition," I said. "Listen first and see." I quickly gave them all the instructions that Johnny had relayed to me. Powy was so slow absorbing it that I had to go through it again. When he nodded to show that he had it straight, I said, "Now, I don't want anything childish like trying to put a couple of men in my car with me. I'm not risking my neck for this. All I want is a hundred-per-cent recovery on the stones so I can pick up my bonus. I'm getting a reward for taking a risk, but I'm not going to make the risk any greater. Powy runs a small-town police department. It isn't big enough or smart enough for Florence City."

"Now, you looka here!" Powy rumbled.

"Please shut up," Guilfarr said. "I agree with Bartells."

I went on. "I want this handled in a big-time way. Let's get a map, a detailed map of that area. That road is eight miles long. They can stop me any place along it. Let's find out how many men Powy can make available, and see where they can be spotted to seal off the area by land and by water. Then orders have got to be clear and specific. Those men are going to have to be brought to their stations after dark, so as not to make our friends suspicious. Another thing, I'm pretty convinced in my own mind that they've been living right here in Florence

City, masquerading as tourists, right along. I can't be seen on the streets today with the law."

Guilfarr nodded. "So far you make sense."

"I know that area pretty well. To get out of the bay, if they use a boat, they'll have to go through either Randolph Pass or Sandy Narrow. Two launches with spots can be moved into position after dark to block the two exits. After dark, men can be moved into the brush to block three roads. The other two will have to be a mobile affair, guys rushed in to block off the other two a reasonable time after I've started my little tour. Seven groups in all. Fourteen good men could handle it, but it would be risky. Twenty would be ideal. Four on the boats, the other sixteen blocking the roads."

"I can arrange that," Powy said.

"Now the dough is going to be a problem," I said, putting a worried tone in my voice. "I get it from the bank at two o'clock. I've got to assume that I may be tailed, and it's going to be damn rough arranging to mark that currency in case they slip through Powy's hands. The split will be about this way: Fifteen hundred hundred-dollar bills, no serial sequence, all used currency; two thousand fifties; and twenty-five hundred twenties. Six thousand separate bills. On used bills you can figure they'll stack at about a hundred to the inch. That'll give you the size of the bundle—a rectangle of eight stacks seven or eight inches deep. Just about the size of a case for a portable typewriter. It'll be wrapped in white cloth so that it won't split when I throw it out. Maybe you could get a man into the bank to see about either recording serial numbers or using one of those infrared dyes or something before I have to pick it up at two o'clock."

Guilfarr seemed to be half asleep. He said, "Rather than take that sort of risk, Bartells, I think we'd best concentrate on sewing up that area so that there'll be no chance of losing the money."

"The company will be very grateful for getting it back," I pointed out. "You see, then there'll be no loss at all on the policy. Even for a big company like ours it means something."

"Of course, of course," Guilfarr said.

I looked at Powy. There was a dew of perspiration on his upper lip in spite of Guilfarr's air conditioning.

"These people are professionals?" Guilfarr asked.

"I'm convinced of it. Usually it's a couple working together, sometimes one, almost never three."

"Odd that they should kill the old lady," Guilfarr murmured.

"It *is* out of character. They usually don't like to make themselves that hot. And there didn't seem to be much point in it. She couldn't have put up much of a fight."

"We want to thank you, Bartells, for seeing your duty as a citizen and for being willing to forget—ah—any ill will you might feel toward the department."

"Thank you, Commissioner."

"If this goes well we may wish to reconsider your resignation of a few years ago."

"Thank you, Commissioner."

He studied me with those green eyes. "I feel that you may have learned something since you've been away from the department. I feel that you may be more—shall we say tolerant, Bartells."

"Any way that I can co-operate . . ."

"Where will you be, Bartells?"

"Mr. Myers will go to the bank with me and then he will have to stay with me until I make the transfer. I imagine he'll insist on riding with me out to where I make the turn. He feels his responsibilities. We'll take the money to the office from the bank, and I imagine he'll want to keep the office open until it's time to go."

"Will you need any police protection while the money is there?"

I showed him the butt of the special. "Both Mr. Myers and I are licensed to carry these, you remember."

"Of course, of course," he murmured. He placed both hands flat on the top of his desk and gave me the smile for the voters. "I really don't think that we need arouse anyone's suspicion by contacting you again. You go through the routine just as you have told us you would. Chief Powy and I will see that there is no slip-up. You can depend on us, Bartells."

They both smiled me to the door. At the door I paused with my hand on the knob. "By the way, Commissioner, Miss Chance would appreciate it if Mrs. Franklin could be released to help her with Mrs. Stegman's personal belongings. Are there any charges?"

Guilfarr raised a questioning eyebrow at Powy.

"They put her in the hospital wing for observation. Far as I know, she's O.K. She was booked on an open charge. We'll make it disturbing the peace and let her go if you say so, Commissioner."

Guilfarr gave me a surprisingly brilliant smile. "Glad to co-operate, Bartells."

"Thank you, Commissioner."

When Harry Banson answered his phone, I hung up and hurried out there and parked in front of the small white frame house.

He stared at me through the screen. "Damn it to hell, Cliff! Why are you parking right in front of—"

I pulled the screen open. "Relax. The Commissioner and I are like this."

He backed away and let me in. Angela came running out of the kitchen, shrieking, "Cliff! Oh, Cliff!" She held my hand hard in both of hers. She looked wonderful, the tears spilling over her eyelids. "Cliff, Ah'm all well! Ah'm home!"

Harry stood beaming at us, his eyes suspiciously moist.

The phone rang and he went and got it. I talked softly to Angela, and she babbled about how wonderful it was to be back and how Harry had met her and about the plane ride. I could hear the hard note of excitement in Harry's voice as he talked into the phone.

He came back out into the hall. "Run along a minute, Angie."

She gave him a dubious look and went back into the kitchen, glancing back at us with a puzzled expression. Harry's nails made a wiry sound against his bristly chin as he scratched and kneaded it. "Now I can figger how they love you all of a sudden."

"So?"

He studied me. "It don't sound right, somehow. It don't sound like you."

"Everybody gets smart sooner or later."

"I heard that Bobby and Nick worked you over. They sure enjoyed it. I didn't figure you to fold after a little workout like that."

He went after something caught in a back tooth with a black-rimmed fingernail, never taking his eyes off me.

"What are they giving you?" I asked.

"They didn't say. I got to go down there."

"Harry, I came out here for one thing. And God help me if I'm wrong. I know how rough things have been. And I know how you've handled yourself. I'm just saying one thing—and one thing only. This is going to be a hell of a poor time to lower your sights, Harry."

He looked at me and the confusion was etched deeply on his face. "I know what you're trying to say, but I can't figure how—"

"Don't try to figure it, Harry. Just do a cop's job in a good cop's way."

The slow grin came. And then he giggled, a surprising whinnying sound. "I don't know how, but I'm too damn happy about thinking about all the things that could happen to be sore at you for thinking that I'd . . ."

"Don't go holy on me. There can always be a first time for everybody, especially if it looks very safe and very easy and everybody is getting theirs and you're the only one left out."

We went out into the kitchen and talked some more and then Harry had to leave. The grouchy sister was gone, and already the towheaded kids were beginning to lose that wary look they'd acquired during the long absence of Angie.

At a quarter of twelve I drove back into town. I thought of Melody, and of her instinct for rebellion. I cruised by the hotel, circled the block, gave up, and parked.

She answered the house phone immediately. "Darling!" she said.

"You're being good? You're staying in there?"

Her voice was mock humble. "I have my orders, don't I?"

"I could come up and steal your clothes to make sure."

"Fascinating idea! Hurry up here!"

The line went dead. I went up to the room. I knocked.

"Who is it?"

"Cliff, of course!"

"Sorry, but I can't let anyone in." I heard her laugh and then she flung the door open and catapulted into my arms, still laughing, the silvery hair tickling my face and throat.

I made her sit down. She put on a solemn childish look. "Did anyone try to see you, Melody?"

"Furny phoned. He apologized for the way he acted the other day. He said that he must have been half crazy with disappointment. He told me that he was just trying to frighten me. He said that he knows that I couldn't have had anything to do with Aunt Elizabeth's death. He sounded very humble. He wanted to come up here and talk to me. I told him no. Then he got very silly. He got all choked up."

"Don't fall for his act. Keep him out of here."

She stood up quickly. "Cliff. Let me be serious. I'm going half crazy wondering about you. You can't let anything happen to you. I'll be corny. I lost Dave. I thought my heart would never mend. But it did, finally. But it couldn't mend twice."

"It'll be over soon."

She stamped her foot. "*Nothing* you have to do can be that important. Whatever it is, give it up! It's me—Melody—asking my man. Asking Cliff. Saying please."

"I'm in too far to stop now. And for the first time I'd be glad to stop."

"Money will buy you out of anything. And I have money. Or I soon will have. I talked to Rainey on the phone. He's leaving this afternoon. He'll have that codicil set aside. I have to use a different law firm to do that. He says that it's only a matter of a few months. Can't we buy you out of this trouble, whatever it is?"

I took her hands. "No, honey."

She snatched her hands away. "Then get out of here! Go on out and play tin soldier. Go on out and beat yourself on the chest."

I shrugged and went to the door. She caught me at the door. "I didn't mean it. I didn't mean it, Cliff."

"Just keep your fingers crossed. Everything will be fine."

She kissed me, hard. "Be careful. For me."

"I'm indestructible."

I pulled the door shut and waited until I heard the clatter of the cross chain. I tried to shake her out of my mind. It was no good. She was stuck there. Tightly. Forever. Half brat and half angel. Domineering, lusty, sensitive, eager, imaginative. Life with her was going to be an emotional roller coaster. And I knew that I wanted a long fast ride.

And if the little men with the horseshoes decided to

cross me up, the only part of her I would take out of life would be the ever vivid memory of one Sunday. And how many people ever carry even that much away with them?

Rainey was in the grillroom. He nodded to me and motioned me over. He was just ordering. I sat down in the booth opposite him.

He coughed and squirmed, intensely embarrassed. "Mr.—uh—Bartells, I've been talking with Miss Chance."

I wanted to help the guy. All I could do was wait, with an attentive expression.

"She told me the glad news. I mean—you and she—"

"If you're congratulating me, thanks."

He pulled at his collar and swallowed. "She has no one, you know. I felt it my duty to act as a—as an adviser. You'll forgive me, I'm sure. Emotional upset. Uh—time to acquire stability. Very important, you know. I told her it would be wiser to wait a few months to be sure, rather than to rush—ah—into a hasty marriage with someone we . . . have just met." He was gasping like a fish out of water and his eyes were agonized. "With the money, it's hard to tell what . . ."

I wanted to pat his hand and comfort him.

"Mr. Rainey, you are a very nice guy. Melody and I are fond of you. I know what you're going to do as soon as you get back. You're going to feel it your duty to get a complete agency report on me. Five pages of single-spaced typewritten dirt. I'll tell you right now. That report will give you plenty of ammunition to go to work on Melody with. It'll be a nice effort and you'll feel better for having made it. And it's going to be O.K. with me for you to try. Now I've got a request for you. Can you stay over a couple of days?"

"Why, I don't know, I . . ."

"Suppose I tell you Melody might need a helping hand, badly, in the next forty-eight hours."

"Then of course I'll stay," he said firmly.

"Now let's eat."

Arthur was tap dancing by the vice-president's desk behind the low oak fence when I went into the bank. His complexion was like fresh window putty.

I pushed the gate open and went back. The VP pressed a button on his desk and nodded to me. He pushed the form over to Arthur, saying, "Now if you'll please sign that, Mr. Myers."

Arthur made his flowing signature as the guard came from the back of the bank with the canvas sack. I put the suitcase Arthur had brought on the edge of the desk and opened it. The sack of money was dumped in and we pressed the cover down until it clicked. Arthur looped the chain around the handles, and then his hand was shaking so badly he couldn't lock it around his wrist, and I had to do it.

"We can supply a guard," the VP said.

"Not necessary," I told him, and shushed Arthur. Already the front doors of the bank were locked, with the guard standing by to let the last customers out.

It was three blocks from the bank to the office. Arthur walked in the middle of the sidewalk, his eyes darting nervously from side to side. It was a respectable piece of change.

15

KATHY and Andrew Hope Maybree stayed with Arthur and me after office hours. The money had been counted, wrapped in white sheeting, and stowed in Arthur's safe.

It was painfully obvious that Kathy was not speaking to Maybree. Her face had settled into sullen lines that looked habitual. Her little body seemed to be sagging with a weariness that was more of the soul than of the muscles.

The four of us sat around, and whenever the big clock on the wall made an electric one-minute jump, we all started.

Kathy sighed and went to her desk and dug out some papers and began typing. Her brown fingers flew over the keys with machine-gun speed. I hitched my chair over next to Maybree's. He gave me a look of quiet disgust.

"Go on," I said in a low tone to him, "keep being a doormat. Keep begging and pleading. I like to see it. She'll keep brushing you off forever."

"It was you all the time," he said in a low tone. "You, damn you! Not me."

Arthur stared at us, his little mouth open.

"Go get a drink of water, Arthur," I told him. He got up obediently and went over to the inverted bottle in the corner.

"Not me either, Maybree. Use your head. With her it was just time going by too fast. We've been good pals, she and I. But not the way you're thinking. Now she's got to be pushed around a little. What are you going to do? Take a stab at it for luck, or let her go out of the picture for keeps?"

It worked on him like one of those sagging little wooden dogs where you push the button on the bottom of the pedestal. Slowly his shoulders straightened and his chin came up. His chest swelled and his eyes narrowed.

"Right now," I said. "Go to it."

He stood up and stalked over to Kathy. Arthur came back and sat down. "What's going on here in my office?"

"Don't interfere, Arthur."

She wouldn't look up at him. She kept typing. "Kathy!" he roared at her, so loudly that Arthur nearly fell off his chair. Kathy stared up at him.

"I want to talk to you!" he said, grabbing her by the wrist.

He dragged her out of the chair and she squealed and tried to bite the back of his hand. He cuffed her upright and yanked her into my office. The door slammed behind them but the light didn't go on.

Her voice came to us, shrill and excited, then abruptly interrupted. Once Arthur winced at the ringing impact of open palm on flesh. His voice was loud at first and then it slowly grew so quiet that we couldn't hear it any more.

The silence lasted. Then the office door opened and they came out. Maybree had his chin up and he wore the conqueror's smile. He tugged Kathy along behind him. The sullen look was all gone from her face. Her dark eyes were aglow.

Maybree marched over to us. "Arthur," he said, "Kathy and I are going to have to have time off for a honeymoon. Ten days will be enough, starting a week from today."

Kathy looked up at Maybree, her eyes adoring.

"Why—ah—sure!" Arthur said.

Maybree turned and patted Kathy on the shoulder. "See? It's all set. Now go back and finish your work, dear."

"Yes, Andrew," she said softly.

Andrew glanced at the clock and cleared his throat sententiously. "Men, I think we should get under way. Kathy, I'll be back to pick you up."

As Arthur went to get the money out of the safe I looked over at Kathy, her head bent obediently over the keys, and I felt oddly sad at something that had been almost mine and now was forever lost. But she and I would have been misery for each other. Now her world would be bright. From now on I would be a mistake, cleverly avoided. Carriages and diapers and play pens and a trick bottle warmer for the six-o'clock feeding. I hoped none of them would inherit Andy's teeth.

Arthur started to sweat again as he came out with the white package. He rode with me, the package between us. Andrew followed us in his car. I pulled up a few hundred yards from where 808 turns right. Fast traffic hummed by.

Andrew stood in the shadows beside Arthur Myers as I put the cross of tar tape on my right headlight.

When I straightened up I saw that Arthur was holding his automatic in his hand. He laughed with harsh, unreal joviality. "Cliff, boy, we won't have to go looking for you south of the border, I hope?"

"Point that damn thing down at your own feet, Arthur."

"You've still got ten minutes, Cliff," Maybree said. "You better head back now."

"Come right to the office, Cliff," Arthur said with a quaver in his voice. "Right to the office. We'll check the stuff against the inventory."

I got behind the wheel. The white package was beside me on the seat. When I was a hundred feet down the highway I saw Andrew swing around in a U turn and head back for the city. I still didn't like my odds. Any part of them. If no murder has been involved, you can feel fairly safe on a purchase. If you're known, you can meet the boy face to face for the switch. But this one was sour. There was nothing more for my unknown friends to lose. A neat little hole in my head and they keep both the dough and the stones. But that was what my bonus was for. The risk of that hole in the head. And if it went like glass, there would be certain other parties eager to make up for the oversight.

At the corner I turned and pulled up. The dashboard clock was accurate at three minutes to nine. I put the special between my thighs very gently. It was on full cock, and the brass under the hammer was alive.

Relax, Bartells. Johnny's sure they're pros. They can't risk crossing you. The grapevine will have them pinned down by name in no time, and they'll never make another sale. They know that too.

Thinking is no good now. See that minute hand? Get the heap rolling. That's it. Now ten miles an hour. Right on the button. Careful, Bartells. Your hands are pretty greasy on that wheel.

The gravel rolled slowly back under the wheels and the headlights waved up and down as the front wheels bounced over the cross ruts. I picked the special out of my lap and held it in my right hand, steering with my left. The right window was down. My right ear itched. I had the crazy idea that it itched right where the slug would hit. At that range I'd never hear the sound of the shot.

The hardest thing I ever did was to keep from pushing down on that gas pedal. I teased it along at ten miles an hour.

One mile, two, three through the night, trees leafed together overhead, blotting out the stars, the headlights shining down the dark tunnel.

Fifty yards ahead a flashlight blinked twice. I shoved the shift up into second with the heel of the hand that held the gun. The car walked, complaining, at five miles an hour. It walked slowly on by where the light had been. 'Way beyond where the light had been.

I gasped with the shock as the hard package hit my arm. It was plain damn fool luck that my finger didn't clamp on the trigger. I jammed on the brake and sat for an instant, breathing hard. I pulled the shift into neutral and down into low, my foot on the clutch. I transferred the special to my left hand, found the package with my right. It weighed about a pound and a half, a chamois bag with a drawstring. I worked my fingers into the neck of it, pulled out a ring. The dash lights hit the stone and refracted into a hard rainbow gleam. I stuffed it back in the sack, put the gun in my lap, picked up the white bundle, and chucked it out through the window, using my wrists, the way you thow a basketball. Over the hum of the motor I heard it crash in the brush.

I sat still and sweat ran into my left eye, acid and stinging. I heard a rattle of the brush and then nothing more. A mosquito, out of season, whined around my ear.

The instant the harsh white beam of the flashlight struck me, I stepped down on the gas and let the clutch out fast. The wagon leaped ahead, the back tires skidding on the gravel. I let the hammer down with my thumb and stuffed the special back into the spring. The car slewed on the next turn and I fought it back. Just as it straightened out, under control, I heard a thin popping sound back where the transfer had been made. Five distant shots and silence, then one more. The boys had wasted no time.

At the end of 808 I turned right as directed, slammed on the brakes, and skidded on dry pavement toward the sawhorse across the road. I ducked below the window level, yanking out the special.

Harry's voice called softly, "Cliff? That you, Cliff?"

I sat up, weak with relief. "Me, Harry. This where they stuck you?"

"Out in left field," he said. He carried the rifle through the crook of his arm.

"Did you hear the shots?" I asked him.

"Listen," he said. I cut the motor. We both heard the thin distant cry of a siren in the night. He laughed without humor. "I'll wait like a good boy until they come and tell me to go home. You go ahead. Take the shoulder and you can get around O.K."

"Be good, Harry," I said.

Arthur was staring down the stairs as I went up, three at a time. When he saw the bag in my hand his smile started to grow. It spread all over his face.

"Good boy! Good boy, Cliff!"

Maybree still hadn't returned from taking Kathy home. We went into Arthur's office and locked the door. I dumped the contents of the bag on his green desk blotter. The collection winked and glittered with an evil fire of its own. Diamond and emerald bracelets, sunburst diamond brooches, pins and clips and rings. Decorations for aged sagging flesh, puffy fingers, dough-soft wrists. The rubies had the gleam of blood.

Arthur's fingers danced over them like little white fat legs and I could hear his breath wheeze in his throat. As he identified each piece he ticked it off on the inventory with a bookkeeper's check mark.

The last item was the diamond that had been pried out of the gold locket.

He looked close to tears of happiness as he said, "All here, Cliff. All here. Everything."

We put it all back in the bag and put it in the safe. He spun the big dial. He patted his comfortable little stomach and danced behind the desk. He stopped suddenly and peered at me. "You look funny!"

"I am a very funny fellow. A natural humorist. Master of the quip."

"O.K. Be snotty. You make more money in one day than I make in five years. Go and laugh yourself to death. But don't tell anybody. You know the company policy. When we make a recovery, it's our own business. You're leaving town tonight, I guess."

"Why should I do that?"

His eyes widened and he jigged nervously. "I don't know what's going on. Something funny. You ought to go away for a while. We've got the stones back. That's all I care."

I went out to the switchboard, changed the night plug to Wilma's line, and phoned the hotel. Melody answered after a long time. Her voice was slurred a bit.

"Progress report, darling," I said. "Now I could almost buy insurance. Almost, but not quite."

"Are you coming over?"

"Not tonight. Go to sleep and dream of me."

Her voice was small and shy. "I could dream better if you were here. Listen to me! I told you I was a no-good woman."

"That hotel gets pretty stuffy about things like that."

"Please tell me how you would have acquired that interesting morsel of information. Who was she?"

"She sold power shovels, sang baritone, and wore Queen Mary hats."

She sighed into the phone. "You're all through now, Bartells. Ball and chain. No more freedom. 'Night, darlin'. Phone me in the morning."

I went directly to headquarters. The fantastic building was aglow with light.

Al Case, the police reporter for the *Messenger,* was leaning against the wall outside Powy's office, sulking. He stared hard at me. He grumbled, "God knows what's going on. A fat lot of co-operation I get around here. Eleven years doing their dirty work, getting their pictures in the paper, and when something pops, a new stiff going into the ice chest, everybody running around tearing the hair off their chests, do they say, 'Let's give the news to good old Al?' In a pig's upper plate they do!"

I pushed into Powy's office. Guilfarr and De Rider were with Powy. All three men looked at me and Powy rumbled, "Don't you know how to knock on a door?"

"Gee, I'm sorry," I said. "I guess I was too excited to think."

"Quite all right, Bartells," Guilfarr said, glaring at Powy. "We want to tell you what happened. First, did you get your stones back?"

"All of them, checked with the inventory."

"Excellent! Excellent!" he assumed a doleful look. "I am afraid that our success doesn't quite measure up to yours."

"They got away!"

"Heavens, no! There were two of them. The man is dead and the woman is in the hospital. Bob Gilman is in the hospital too, with a smashed knee. The group that contacted the couple was composed of Chief Powy, Gilman, and De Rider here. Chief, suppose you tell Clifford what happened."

"We had men posted all around the area the way you suggested, Bartells. At eight o'clock the three of us took a car back into the groves, and then we went up on foot, being as careful as we could. We stopped about a hundred yards shy of the road and about two miles in from the highway. Right after nine you came along. We saw the cross on the headlight. When you'd gone by we knew they were in farther, so we got out in the road and came along after you. I'm carrying too much weight to make good time, so Gilman and De Rider went on ahead of me. You fill in, Nick."

De Rider gave me a quick look. "We were beginning to get pretty bushed when we saw the light blink 'way ahead of you. We slowed down then and came on careful-like. When you stopped, we stopped. We saw the money when you tossed it out and we moved up close. When you gunned it and took off, we went in fast. Gilman had the big flashlight and he was swinging it back and forth to catch them. Soon as I saw the shadows of them there, I let fly and saw one of them go down. I didn't know until later it was the woman. I sure didn't want to shoot any woman. Well, right then Gilman went down, yelling he'd been shot. The guy took off through the brush, me after him."

"But he got away from you in the dark?" I asked politely.

De Rider coughed nervously. "Now, that's just what he did. I sure lost him. I circled around but I couldn't pick him up again. I went back to where Gilman was. The Chief came up and pretty soon the sedan came over because the boys had heard all the shooting. The Chief called in for an ambulance for Bob and the woman. The Chief told me to go back after the car we'd come in. I hiked back down the road and I got the other sedan to take it back to town. As I got to the edge of the groves I saw a shadow and I swung and caught it in the headlights. Soon as I did that, he let fly a shot and ducked back into the groves. I swung and chased him with the car. I just wanted to make him give up. I fired in his general direction and . . ."

"Unfortunately got him in the heart? Or was it the head?"

"Right through the head," Chief Powy said. "Damn miserable luck. You see, Bartells, while he was dodging around in there he stashed that money someplace. He had time to bury it or stuff a rock in it and sink it in one of those pools. We've left Harry there to guard the entire area until morning, when we can make a regular hunt for it. But I'm sure afraid we're going to have trouble—yes, sir, a lot of trouble—finding out what he did with it. Hadn't been for Nick's bad luck with that shot, he could have told us himself."

"Is the woman hurt badly?" I asked.

"She got it in the shoulder. She'll be all right. The doc says she can answer questions in the morning."

"You won't mind if I ask her some questions, too, will you? Just for the company records. Red tape. You know how it is."

Powy looked questioningly at Guilfarr. The Commissioner shrugged. "I can't see anything wrong with that. After we talk to her in the morning, that is. On your way out, Bartells, please tell Al Case to come in. It will be all right with you to give him the full story?"

"Leave my name and the name of the company out of it, Commissioner. Matter of policy. Just say it was a representative of the estate trying to buy back the stones who co-operated with the police on setting the trap for the thieves."

"Sure thing," the Commissioner said with a smile.

"Too bad about the money," I said.

Powy looked sympathetic. "A damn shame."

16

I SAT AT THE END of the corridor the next morning and chatted with an intern and a nurse with the giggles while the police group was in with Mrs. Frey.

They were taking a long time. "Will she be in shape to talk to me?" I asked.

"Sure," the intern said. "That woman has a lot of vitality. She'll mend fast. Nice-looking, too. You just can't figure people, can you?"

"How's her attitude?"

"What do you expect? She's pretty bitter. Her husband's dead. She's facing a hell of a long prison term when she recovers. She isn't what you'd call cheery. Would you be?"

The nurse went off into another gale of giggles. That intern was killing her. They beamed at each other.

I looked down the hall as the group came out. Powy's face was an angry brick red. He glared at me as I approached. "Go in and have a nice chat, Bartells," he said. "Go in and get real chummy."

"You didn't get anything?"

"I'm glad we got the name they were living under. If we hadn't traced their car back and found out they stayed at the Pelican House, I wouldn't even know that much."

The nurse swept by me with a crisp rustle. I followed her in. "Are we comfortable, Mrs. Frey? Is there anything I can get you?"

The woman on the bed had dark hair, a strong handsome face, a band of white running through her hair at the left temple. She looked at me rather than at the nurse. She rolled her head back and stared up at the ceiling. The shoulder and arm had already been placed in a cast. It looked lumpy and uncomfortable.

"Shut the door on the way out," I told the nurse.

She rustled out and closed the door quietly. The room still stank of Powy's cigar. I pulled a chair over close to the bed, sat down, and lit two cigarettes. I put one between the fingers of her left hand. She raised it slowly to her lips. But she didn't look at me.

"The best thing you can do is keep your mouth shut when they come around," I said. "Talking to the law won't do you any good."

She turned her head and looked at me. The dark eyes were bottomless. "You say," she murmured.

"I say. You and your man hit a sour one. As sour as they come. It could have been a breeze."

She sucked on the cigarette again, exhaled slowly toward the ceiling. "When you're casing them, they're all breezes, friend."

"You're no punk kid. And I don't think your man was. I think you both knew how to handle yourselves. It smelled funny to me from the beginning. Where did it go off the rails?"

"I don't know what you're talking about."

"Didn't you have a hunch this one would turn sour, Mrs. Frey?"

"I'd like to go back to sleep, copper."

"I'm no copper. I'm checking for the insurance company. The room isn't wired for sound. Anything you tell me you can deny. It's just you and me."

"The insurance company! A nice cross. Bartells, they tell us. If you want to sell, go through Alfrayda to Bartells. Dandy!"

"That only goes for the pros, honey. Not fumblers. Not people knocking off old ladies."

I saw her fingers squeeze the end of the cigarette into a thin wet line. "Not us. We handled our end."

"You fumbled it. You got excited and fumbled it."

Her mouth took on an ugly twist. "He's dead now. Wally's dead. Dead because we were crossed."

I leafed through the mental card file. Wally. A faint

and distant bell rang. An almost legendary couple. Wally and Bea. Something about a very big one in Paris right after the war.

"You and Wally should have stuck to the Continent, Bea."

Sticking a pin in her arm would have had the same effect.

"Who are you?" she whispered.

"The guy who can let the word get out that you two fumbled it. Or maybe I'm the guy who can find out more about the old lady."

"Then you can't be a cop. They won't worry about the old lady any more. Not with Wally dead and me on the string."

"The more I have to go on, the better I can do."

She dropped the cigarette over the side of the bed. "Light me another."

I handed it to her. "Here it is. But I'll deny every damn word of it," she said. "Wally made the contact with that Franklin. It looked good. We made the contact in October, and we wanted to pull it in Boston. Things didn't shape up right. We had to come down here. I wanted to give up and find a new one to work on, because I didn't like that Franklin the one time I met him. Wally said it would be even easier down here. We were down to our last couple of thousand. We had to live cheap down here. Franklin got the key to us and we got the duplicate made. The old lady went to bed early. Franklin got the combination of the safe. He didn't have the nerve to do it himself. There was a big party on at one of the other apartments downstairs in that Tide Winds. A good night for it. We wouldn't be noticed coming and going by anyone.

"We went in a little after ten. She was snoring. A real easy one. We got the gag in her mouth and the wrists and ankles tied and a bandage around her eyes. She never saw us. The safe opened on the first try. We cleaned it out and left the cash. The cash was Franklin's end. The way it was supposed to work, with the bedroom door shut, he would be the one to find her, still tied up, in the morning. She wouldn't be able to see him. He had some place, I guess, where he was going to hide the cash, in the spare tire of the Buick or something. His wife wasn't in on it. He was supposed to untie her and yell for the cops. We weren't in her place over six minutes. Nobody paid any attention to us, going or coming. We went back to our place and looked the stuff over and had a drink and went to bed.

"The next morning we're eating breakfast when it comes over the radio. What a mess! We couldn't figure it. It made no sense. Then we decided that maybe Franklin had come back earlier to check and somehow the old lady had gotten the bandage off her eyes. We were never in a murder deal before. We couldn't run because we didn't have the money. We had to sit and go crazy just thinking about it.

"Then a few nights later Franklin comes over. Some guy is after him. Some guy has talked to his wife. He's scared to death. We've got to give him some of the stuff, he says. He's leaving the country. We knew he'd be picked up. We knew that if he was picked up, he'd bring us into it, and we knew that once we were in it, our record was so much against us we'd be all through forever. In the meantime we'd been up to Tampa and made a contact with Alfrayda. When Franklin came around in the middle of the night, Wally took him for a walk to talk things over. He didn't tell me, but I sort of imagined what he would do. He came back trembling so bad he couldn't even speak. He'd used a piece of broken cinder block and dumped Franklin into the water. Franklin was our only contact and he was dead. I pleaded with Wally. I told him we had to drop the hot stuff in the bay, off the bridge or something, and get out, even if we had to hitchhike, but he thought we could come out right on it and do it in such a way nobody would grab us.

"I threw the stuff into the car. The money came out and Wally checked it. I shined the light and the car went away. The next thing I knew, people yelled and something hit me on the shoulder and I couldn't see or hear. I was on the ground and I wasn't out completely. Just almost. There was a siren and then a needle in my arm and I woke up here this morning in this cast and they told me Wally is dead. You're right. It was sour. All the way. But the old lady—no, we didn't."

She closed her eyes. Her features were placid with exhaustion, with emotional release.

I stood up. "That's enough to go on, Bea. I'm going to see if I can clear you of the old lady's death. Franklin's death will be marked up to Wally. Maybe you'll get off with as little as five."

She opened her eyes and looked up at the ceiling. She smiled. "Me, a tramp from Troy, New York. I was with him three years before I found out he wasn't spending dough his dad had left him. He taught me to put it on for the people. The right accent and the right words. He was a funny-looking little guy. When I found out what he was, it was join him or leave him, and it was too late to leave him. Do you think I care whether it's five years or fifty? Get out now. I'm going to sleep."

I went out into the corridor and shut the door behind me. The nurse was down by the desk still giggling. I thought of a crook, a funny-looking little guy, standing in a flashlight's beam, his trembling hands in the air, his woman unconscious and bleeding on the ground. I saw him, the money on the ground beside him where he had dropped it.

Then the whip crack of the shot, but he didn't hear it because the slug was smashing through his head by then. A little man standing quick trial by the side of a dark road, found guilty because of what was on the ground beside him, wrapped in white.

Then the whispers, because guilt always whispers, even when there is no one to hear. The debate. Give it to her, too? A good idea. But no one quite able to pull the trigger. Hell, she was out like a light. How would she know he didn't run off with the dough? Everybody relieved to have it settled.

And leave good old Harry to guard the place where the money isn't.

The best way to learn how a cat will jump is by living with cats for a while. They had jumped the way I thought they would. But they didn't know it yet. They were mentally spending the money. Those fine unmarked bills. One hundred to the inch. Enough for you and you and you and you. Plenty, this time, boys. And the first one of you bastards gets dumb, blossoms out with a big car or a blonde in mink, you maybe get accidentally shot in line of duty. Now Gilman. One extra grand to him on account of me shooting him in the leg so as to make it look good for us to be shooting at the couple. He knows the last thing I wanted to do was get the knee.

The nurse rustled up so close to me I could smell her

breath. It was peppermint. "She's going to sleep," I said.

The nurse nodded. "She'll be a good patient. Funny, isn't it? The ones with nothing are the good patients. When they come in with quilted bed jackets and ivory radios to have ingrown toenails worked on, then you've got to watch them. They want a nurse every second to wait on them."

I gave her my card. "Here. Anything she wants extra, I'm good for it. Scotty, down at the desk, knows me. Tell her. You've got a boy in here I wonder about. Kreshak. Know anything?"

"Men's ward, that one. He goes out today. He's the one who always wants to have somebody combing his hair. He gives me the creeps."

I patted her starchy shoulder. "If you have to comb it again, you've got my permission to use a chair leg."

The gag was no good, but according to the giggles that followed me down the corridor, I was working on her bare foot with a feather.

I went out into the sunlight, but Bea had taken the gold out of it. Get out the books and add up the columns and say, "This woman has sinned against her fellow humans. She has broken the laws of God and the laws of the state. This is her just desert." You can balance the books that way, but it does nothing to take away the memory of bottomless dark eyes, of a tired voice saying, "Five or fifty."

The next stop was the hotel. It had been worth an extra edition. The papers were racked by the newsstand. "POLICE TRAP MURDERERS"; "STEGMAN KILLERS IN GUN BATTLE"; "KILLER SLAIN, COMPANION INJURED"; "GEMS RECOVERED, MONEY MISSING."

I took a copy and sat down in the lobby and skimmed through it. The handling was fine. The statement of what had happened was a direct quote from Commissioner Guilfarr.

My end of it was neatly handled. It was covered in one sentence. "The trap was set when the Frey couple made contact with a representative of the estate, offering to sell back the stones for a substantial payment in unmarked currency."

Powy was quoted in words he would never have used: "It is indeed unfortunate that Frey eluded pursuit just long enough to conceal the money, but there is every hope that the hiding place will soon be discovered."

The most tragic and comic aspect was covered in another paragraph. "The entire area where the gun battle took place has been sealed by the police and an intensive search has been planned, utilizing volunteers from the American Legion Post and also Troops 3, 18, and 61 of the Boy Scouts, who have been excused from school today in order to participate."

As I stood up and tossed the paper on the chair, there was a discreet cough behind me. I turned and looked into Trumbull's deeply tanned face.

"I've been hoping to run into you, Mr. Bartells."

We smiled at each other like a pair of rival car dealers waiting for the luncheon meeting to start.

"I'm afraid I made a bit of an exhibition of myself the other day. The way it has all turned out, I'm afraid Melody will never forgive me for the things I said to her after I found that silly ring." His voice turned husky. "But when a man sees the one girl in the world slipping away . . . I guess you can't hold him accountable, can you?"

"Did you come here to see her?"

He shrugged. "She's still annoyed with me. She wouldn't come down to the lobby and she wouldn't let me go up. Very discouraging."

"You haven't given up?"

"Why, of course not! She'll forgive me sooner or later. We have the same background, you know. A great deal in common. Our tastes are the same." He coughed as though embarrassed. "And she *does* like lovely and expensive things. She's been denied them for years. And the terms of the will, of course . . ." His voice trailed off.

"Of course," I said, mocking him gently, "the terms of the will. Dear old Aunt Elizabeth's wishes."

"I've been trying to like you, Bartells. But you *do* make it difficult."

"Forget me. What is the song and dance you want to give Melody?"

"Isn't it obvious? I was still in a state of emotional shock at Elizabeth's murder. My judgment wasn't too good. I really didn't think Melody had anything to do with it, but it seemed a good idea at the time to try to frighten her into marrying me."

"You'd be in a wonderful spot, Trumbull, if Melody dropped dead."

"You *are* coarse, Bartells. Do you really think that money would mean anything to me in a world without her?"

"Do you write those lines, or do you hire a guy?"

He shifted a little onto the balls of his feet. He looked as if he would be very rough. A natural athlete, a man with nothing better to do for the last fifteen years than keep himself in shape. The anger went out of him.

"There isn't much use talking to you, Bartells."

"Now, that's where you're wrong. I'm the good fairy, ready to tie a ribbon in your curly brown locks. I'm always on the side of true love. I like to see a man get a chance to tell his story. And Melody needs a change of scene. If nothing interferes, I think I'll take her on a beach picnic tomorrow. If you could sort of casually drop around . . ."

He was wary about the teeth on the gift horse. "Where would that be?"

"A little sand spit with about five palms on it. It's called Coquina Island. It's out opposite Marlow Beach, about four miles out. At the Marlow Beach pier you can hire a launch to run you out and pick you up any time you say."

"When do you plan to get there?"

"About ten-thirty in the morning. If you came about eleven-thirty . . . After all, how can she avoid you on an island a quarter-mile long and a hundred yards wide?"

"Just the two of you?" he asked.

"Just the three of us, if you show up. I'm going to try hard to make it. It all depends on whether a certain, uh, business arrangement interferes. You could call it an appointment."

He stuck his hand out and showed his teeth. "Old man, maybe I have made the wrong decisions about you."

I shook hands with a childish desire to cross the fingers of my other hand.

After I watched him leave the lobby, pause in the sun, and then head slowly off to the left, I went to the house phones and called Melody.

Her voice had the glitter of ice in it. "Do come up, Cliff."

The first thing I saw when I walked into her room was

the paper on the bed. The moment I shut the door behind me she pointed to the paper and said, "Hah! A representative of the estate, are you? I know darn well it wasn't Rainey."

Her eyes had gone almost as green as Guilfarr's. She wore a brown linen dress and a wide red Mexican belt, studded with red, blue, and yellow glass gems. She had both hands on her hips in fishwife stance, her shoulders thrust forward, her foot tapping ominously.

"All right, I was the little man who was there on the scene."

"You big fool! You big stupid! Who were you showing off for? That little piece that works in your office? Those people were killers. They'd proved that. And so you went off into the brush and played decoy for the police force. A gun battle! Just for the sake of a lot of jewelry that belongs to me! Did it ever occur to you, friend, that I don't think the jewelry is more important than you?"

I went to her and put my hands on her wrists. I put both her hands behind her and caught both the wrists in my left hand. She began to squirm. I kissed her and she tried to bite me. I swept the silvery-gold hair across her face and she stamped at my feet with high sharp heels. I shook her until her face was a blur and until she went soft and fell against my chest, moaning softly.

I kissed her again. "Better," I said. "Much more reasonable."

"Oh, Cliff!"

"Sit down over there and I'll be 'way over here, because I want to talk to you and I can't keep talking if we keep doing this."

She sat by the windows and I pushed the paper aside and sat on the bed.

"I don't know enough about Aunt Elizabeth."

"What!"

"I want to know more about her. What would it take to panic her?"

She gave me a lopsided grin. "The H bomb might do it. I don't think so, though. She had more iron determination than the Marine Corps."

"Was she pretty agile?"

"For her age, very. Why all this, Cliff?"

"Want to go on a beach picnic tomorrow?"

"You ask a stir-crazy girl that?" She pounced from her chair and landed beside me on the bed.

I made a long reach for the bedside phone. I lay face down, propped on my elbows, until Wilma announced that this was indeed the Security Theft and Accident Insurance Company.

"This's Cliff," I said, trying to fend Melody off with an elbow. "I'm at the Coast Hotel. Calls or company?"

"Neither," she said with a note of pleasure. "Your voice sounds funny."

"It should. There's a stupid blonde here chewing on my ear. Ow!"

"Really!" Wilma said huffily. The line clicked dead.

I rolled into a startling agility of brown linen, a laughing froth of gold and silver hair.

17

MELODY AND I had lunch down in the grill at one. We were talking in half sentences, in words that would mean nothing to anybody else in the world. I had discovered that I could see a pulse in her throat and could, by judicious choice of words, speed it up or slow it down at will. It was a good game.

Then the waitress came and asked me if I was Mr. Bartells and told me there was a phone call for me. The call was short and to the point. They gave me a big ten minutes to get over to the county courthouse. I went back and told Melody. I requested that she keep her fingers crossed.

They had done a fast job of collecting an emergency grand jury. It was meeting in Judge March's chambers. Solid citizens. Sober, solid citizens, wearing those expressions of mixed glee and solemnity that result from the disclosure of something really hot.

The gaunt man from the Tampa office was there. He gave me twenty seconds' worth of instructions and led me in. I was seated in an uncomfortable chair facing the long table, sworn in, and told to tell my story.

I spoke my piece like a little man. A little old man with a face like an embittered monkey asked permission to throw a few questions at me.

"When you were on the force, Bartells, did you accept

monies at any time as a bribe for not doing your sworn duties?"

"No, sir."

"Were monies offered you at any time?"

"Not directly, sir. Just through hints."

"Is the rumor true that you were broken as the result of an argument over the division of protection money paid by one Anthony Lavery, straw owner of the Kit-Kat?"

"No, sir. That rumor is not true."

"Is it true that you have aided the federal men in this affair through some idea of revenging yourself against the men who broke you?"

"I can't say that I didn't resent being broken. But I decided to try to nail them to the cross after I took a beating at headquarters last week."

"Do you expect us to believe that you were beaten by officers of the law and yet you made no complaint to anyone in authority?"

"If that's a question, I think it's a little naïve."

Judge March smiled wisely and sourly.

"How much did you get paid for recovering the jewelry, Bartells?"

"I would prefer not to answer that question. I report that to the Bureau of Internal Revenue. I don't think it is anyone's business."

"That's all, Bartells. Thank you."

The gaunt man said, "With your permission, I would like Mr. Bartells to remain here for the demonstration. He may be able to give us advice on the preparation of the warrants."

March nodded and I took a seat over at the side. The gaunt man opened the outer door and nodded. Two serious young men came in. One was the weather-conscious redhead. He went to the table and placed four dollar bills flat against the table at roughly three-foot intervals. The second young man stood waiting, wearing and carrying a man-from-Mars gizmo that looked faintly familiar to me.

The gaunt man said, "With the co-operation of the bank, and the cyclotron technicians at the university, a lead box containing radioactive material was taken to the basement of the bank. The money paid to the thieves by Mr. Bartells was placed in the box and bombarded for a three-hour period, thus imparting to it radioactivity that will last for a period of from two to three weeks. One of those four dollars on the table was also rendered radioactive. Do not move back away from it. It is a low radioactivity, harmless to humans. The young man is carrying a Geiger counter. Watch him carefully."

The room was so still that everyone could clearly hear the intermittent clicking of the counter. As the young man neared the table the thing began to click more frequently. He held it over the bills and the clicks came so fast that there seemed to be no interval between them. He held it close to one bill and then to the second. But when he held it over the third bill, the clicking merged into a roar. He backed away and the clicking died down immediately.

Some of the jurors applauded involuntarily.

The gaunt man said, "That is how we plan to locate the money. Mr. Bartells will help us look in all of the likely places, and warrants can be made out here to give us the right to search those likely places."

"You can come along," the gaunt man said.

"I wouldn't miss it for the world."

We went to the bank first. The Assistant District Attorney was along, his red face shining with excited perspiration. We went to the safety deposit vault. The redhead handled the counter. He found the first box on the left, a big box near the wall.

"Number six-thirty-three," he called.

The bank man checked the file. "John Guilfarr," he said, a tremble in his voice. Papers were passed to the bank man and the box was opened.

"Number four-eighty," the redhead called over the roar of the counter.

"Homer Stackson," the bank man said.

I wondered how Homer got cut in. I watched the box being opened. Poor Homer got only six fifties out of the take.

The numbers were intoned and the names were called out. No Powy, no Gilman, no De Rider. But a very neat cross section of municipal big shots. An interesting list. A list to make wives cry and the kids wonder what the hell had happened to the old man. There'd be some plush homes for sale in Florence City. There would be a new political deal. All because you learn how a cat will jump when it smells raw kidney.

Then the redhead went behind the tellers. The bank customers looked on curiously. The tellers were jumpy. The counter began to shout its head off at window three, over the cash drawer. The bank officer went through the deposit slips. One Nicholas De Rider had put $1,500 into his checking account that morning.

It was a stupid thing to have done, but it turned out to be smart, inadvertently smart. It was laborious sorting out the treated money. The total came to $1,370. The rest had been paid out through the window. A few innocents were walking around with hot money—hot in a brand-new sense of the word.

The next stop was headquarters. Powy was in. His face turned the color of damp ashes. He knew something was wrong, but he couldn't get it through his head exactly what it was. The big iron safe in the corner of his office was supposed to be for police business. The counter roared and roared.

He opened the safe and then decided that he shouldn't have done it and tried to kick it shut. He missed and his foot slipped and he sat down on the office floor, looking like a pudgy gray child about to break into fat tears.

Powy had done very neatly by himself. It was $80,000. Guilfarr was the big boy with $120,000. The remaining $100,000 had been scattered around.

It was a painful job in headquarters. Gowan had his tiny amount in his desk drawer. Some of them had it on them. It was all taken and every man got his summons to appear.

The one I liked best was Nick De Rider. He came swaggering down the corridor and stopped dead. "De Rider," I whispered to the gaunt man.

"You deposited fifteen hundred dollars of the insurance company's money to your account this morning, De Rider," he said.

De Rider grinned. "You gone crazy? That was money I've been saving a long time."

The redhead had gone around behind Nick. He held the counter close to the seat of Nick's pants, and when it roared, Nick jumped as if a bee had stung him. He turned around. "What the hell are you doing, fella?"

"You've got radioactive money in your pants, De

Rider. For your sake, I hope you haven't been carrying it very long. You know how that stuff works."

Nick swallowed hard and his eyes went wide. "Jesus! That money? The money in the bundle?" He clawed the wallet out of his hip pocket and threw it away from him so hard that it hit the corridor wall and slapped to the floor. His voice was high. "I was carrying it around ever since Powy gave it to me last night. What's it going to do to me?"

The gaunt man shook his head and clucked. "That's a long time, De Rider. With immediate treatment maybe we can save your manhood. But I don't see why we should try. You don't look like the sort who'll co-operate with us."

Nick blubbered and looked about to fall on his knees and beg. He had his own style of guts. You could crack his knuckles with a sledge and he'd grin at you and tell you to go to hell. But this was different. This was a threat at the very core of his being.

"Co-operate! Quick, what do you want? Anything you want. Only help me get treated quick."

They took him into an office and one of the gaunt man's boys took the stenotype machine out of its case. Nick jittered on the chair.

"A complete statement, De Rider. Everything. Not only this little caper, but all the rest of the dirt. Lavery's payoffs. Everything you can remember and think of."

The words poured out of him so fast that the stenotype operator had difficulty keeping up. I knew some of the things, without proof. Others I hadn't heard of before.

And a prize tumbled out with all the rest of it. A glittering prize. "That Frey fella," he said. "He didn't have a gun. That made it a little tough. We took one out of our collection here afterwards, one we picked up with no number a couple years ago. When we told him to run he wouldn't. I couldn't do it with him standing there. The Chief took my gun and did it."

"Did he have his orders?"

"I heard Guilfarr tell him before we left to make damn sure."

"We'll have this typed up, and when you sign it we'll rush you to the laboratory and counteract this radiation, if we can," the gaunt man said.

"I'll sign it after. Honest!" Nick wailed.

"We'll do it my way," the gaunt man said.

After the statement was signed, the gaunt man said, "Thanks, De Rider. Now you can relax. That money isn't dangerous. You could wear shorts made of it for the rest of your life and never miss a trick."

They'd taken his gun. He looked at the gaunt man with a dull lack of comprehension. His eyes shifted to me and the hate flowed into them. A deadly and murderous hate.

"You wise bastard," he whispered.

I was still wearing the special. I made the bad mistake of underestimating the speed of his reflexes. He hit me and the gaunt man in a flying block that drove us together out the doorway into the corridor, sliding across the tile floor. As I went through the door I swung my arm for balance and it hit the doorframe, numbing my fingers, sending the special flying.

De Rider turned and half dived for the door, his eye on the weapon. I scrambled after him and got my hands on his ankle, trying to yank him back. But he had caught the edge of the frame in his fingertips. He pulled the two of us forward and grabbed the gun just as I tried to swarm over him and get hold of the wrist.

He rolled and chopped me across the side of the head with the barrel. The whole world faded into swirling gray and I could feel my hands slipping off him. He was gone and I sat up and shook the mist out of my eyes. There was a wetness on the side of my face. The gaunt man was on his feet, his back against the opposite wall of the corridor. De Rider was in a crouch, balanced on his toes, the gun thrust forward, but for some crazy reason it wasn't pointed at me, but at someone down the corridor, cut off from my vision by the edge of the doorframe.

He backed up, one cautious step after another. His lips were pulled back from his teeth. "I don't want to, but I will," he said.

"Drop it, Nick," Harry said scoldingly. "Come on, boy. Be sensible."

"I'm telling you, Banson."

Harry came into sight, the Police Positive in his yellowish hand.

"Stop comin' at me!" Nick yelled.

"Now, boy. No call to act like that."

My gun jumped in Nick De Rider's hand. The little lance of muzzle flame was clearly visible. The shot slammed and rolled and thundered in the corridor. Harry stood his ground and fired calmly. The impact spun Nick around so that he was in profile to Harry. He lifted my gun again and Harry fired first. I knew by the way Nick went down that Harry had done it exactly right, planting the slug low on the outside of the nearest shoe so that it swept both feet out from under De Rider. His head smacked the tile and the gun slid up toward Harry, spinning slowly, coming to rest with the muzzle pointed at the unconscious De Rider.

Harry picked the gun up. He beamed at me. "Hi, there, Cliff! Know what I am? Acting chief. First official act. Tried to teach that boy to shoot a dozen times. He just never had the feeling for it, I guess."

I slowly got to my feet, dabbing at my face with my handkerchief. I froze there as we heard the hollow blam of another shot.

"Busy day," Harry muttered.

It was Powy. He still looked like a fat gray baby. But the nipple of the bottle had been the blue steel muzzle of the gun that should have been taken from him. The gun was in his lap, wedged between the fat thighs, and the back of his head was a scattered substance that slid wetly down the plaster wall behind his desk.

Al Case wandered in, a wide and happy smile on his face, mumbling, "AP, UP, INS, exclusives . . . awp!" The smile slid off his face like butter off a steak. He covered his mouth with his hand, turned, and fled. I couldn't laugh at him. I was too close to following right behind him.

By dusk most of it was cleaned up. Harry Banson had displayed a totally unexpected executive quality. Guilfarr had been tipped, and he was making his run for it. Full descriptions had gone out on the tape. It was a mad tangle at both headquarters and the courthouse. Lawyers shouting about their clients' rights. Protestations of great innocence. "I tell you, Powy owed me a thousand bucks. Can I help it if the bastard paid me in that kind of money? Can I?"

Harry strolled smiling and unruffled through all of it, showing his bad teeth, making phone calls, rebuilding the nucleus of a police force, feeding the right sort of tidbits to the press.

The big black headlines had it in four words: "OFFICIALS COUGH UP SWAG."

There was nothing you could add to that. They had it and they had to cough it up, no matter how it hurt. The grand jury ate at the big table, hasty sandwiches, eating even while they were hearing testimony.

Harry, seemingly in fifty places at once, cornered me on the courthouse steps. "You're deputy chief, boy," he said gently.

"Just like that?"

"You want it, don't you? Come on over. I'll swear you in. And say! Pinch me! Ow! Guess it's for sure."

"Swear me in and don't release it. I've got something to do that I can do as a cop better than as a citizen."

He swore me in with Al Case as a witness. Al was pledged to secrecy. I said the words. Harry frowned. "Al, how the hell much does a deputy chief get?"

Al shrugged. "You should ask me!"

"I got forty-five hundred when I was a lieutenant," I said. "That includes the cost-of-living bonus."

"Give him fifty-five," Al said.

"O.K., Cliff. You're my deputy. Here's your first job: Close up the Kit-Kat."

"Can I come along?" Al pleaded.

"Come on. We'll do it now."

"How many men we taking?"

"Just us, Al. You and me."

He swallowed hard.

The lot was full of cars. My head itched where the doc had shaved it around the gash Nick had made. Larry Kreshak let us go right in. "He's been sort of expecting you," Larry said.

Tony Lavery was in his bedroom tenderly packing a big wardrobe trunk with Havana stickers on it. He gave me a tired smile. "The clown prince," he said.

"Still clowning, too," I said.

Tony lit a cigarette. "For you, Al, I'm saying this. The management has been considering the closing of the Kit-Kat for some time. The decision was made three days ago to close"—he looked questioningly at me—"next Monday?"

"Tomorrow, Tony. Close the tables tonight. Just food and liquor."

He sighed. "O.K. Have it your way. Tomorrow, Prince."

Al looked at me. "I should write it like he says it's going to be?"

"Why not? He's all through here. They're indicting him, but he'll beat it because he doesn't take silly chances. Let him save his face with his own outfit."

"Mix you guys a drink?" Tony asked.

We named our choice and followed him out into the other room. He sipped his drink. "They're sore at me, Prince. I've been on the phone."

"Is it your fault?"

"Anything that goes wrong with the setup is the manager's fault. Maybe I should have siphoned some brains into that crowd over there. Who cares? They'll sell at a profit. There's a good living here just in the food and liquor."

I looked at him. "Tony, you just don't sound sore enough."

Surprisingly, he blushed. "I can't seem to get sore. I'm quitting. I've got a pile. Know what I'm going to do?"

"Those big damn shining buildings, Tony?"

"If I can get in anyplace. First I got to get the high-school credits. Imagine that. Tony Lavery in high school."

I set the empty glass on the desk and stuck my hand out. He gave me a twisted grin and shook it. "You're O.K., Prince. Just too damn Christer."

"Luck, Tony. Lots of luck."

"Tell your blonde to send back them clothes, Prince. Lucy thinks I gave 'em away."

I stood by Al Case out by the pool and I listened to the laughter of the women. A place kicks you and you want to kick back. You want to badly, and then when you get your chance, you're a little sorry.

"What makes you think he won't open the table tonight?" Al demanded.

"He said he wouldn't."

"It beats the hell out of me," Al mumbled.

"What are you going to do now, Al?"

"Turn in some stuff. Then see what makes over at City

Hall. Then clean up some odds and ends. Coupla interviews. Biggest day since VJ day. I'm beat."

I let him off at his office, went back to my room, and phoned Melody. She was in.

"I'm a little smarter than I was, Cliff. You were in on it, weren't you? You helped sew them up. I can understand a little better now."

"What do you eat on picnics?"

"Cold chicken. Mountains of it. Cliff, is there anybody around loose who wants to get even with you?"

"How about this for a menu? A thermos of Martinis, a half bushel of cold chicken, a dozen bottles of beer."

"Where are we going?"

"A small annex just west of heaven."

"Crowds of people?"

"Us. Desolately alone. Like a shipwreck."

"Think we ought to interrupt this honeymoon long enough to get married?"

"It's a thought, sugar. Tomorrow's Wednesday. Thursday I've got to get a haircut. Friday I've got to take a book back to the library. Monday suit you?"

"Fine, unless there's a good movie on."

"We'll get back tomorrow in time for tests and licenses."

"Trapping, baby. Trapping."

I ate the last of my eggs and fell headlong into a dreamless sleep, blacker and more silent than any tomb.

18

SHE WAS IN holiday fettle. I found shade for the big basket of food and the trick container designed to keep the beer cold.

She watched the launch swing away from the island and dwindle off toward the mainland, a dark line on the horizon. The air was cool but the sting had come back into the sunshine.

She wore a halter and shorts. She turned to me accusingly and said, "Oaf! I heard you tell him to come back. I want to be shipwrecked for keeps. Forever."

"Would the food hold out?"

"Don't be so damn practical. Here's a better question: Would you hold out?"

"The implication is resented, madame."

"Shut up. Take me on a tour. I want to explore."

We left our swim suits, coats, shoes, and socks by the food. I rolled up the cuffs of my blue jeans. A complete circuit was only a little more than half a mile, but it took a long time. Every shell had to be identified. I had to find her some scuttling white sand fleas. I found one nearly the size of a mouse, and it horrified her. She exclaimed with joy when a pair of porpoises rolled lazily not over fifty yards away. It was a day to be young and gay in.

She found a place she liked, where the sand was clean and hard-packed.

"Now build me a house," she said.

"I'll build you a Martini."

"Fair exchange."

I lugged all the stuff over while she watched me, saying, "I always take a man on my picnics."

Her drink was half gone when the drone of the approaching launch separated itself from the deep voice of the waves against our beach. She jumped up and ran up the sand slope to where she could see.

"Cliff!" she wailed. "We're going to have people in our hair."

"Take a good look, chum."

As she shaded her eyes, I patted the right-hand pocket that held the Belgian automatic I had taken back from her when I had picked her up at the hotel.

There was both anger and bewilderment in her voice. "It's Furny! How would he . . . Cliff, you asked him to come!"

"Guilty."

She ran back to me, sat on her heels, and stared into my eyes. "Why, Cliff?"

"Because it will feel so good when he goes away."

"Tell me now. We haven't much time. They're getting close."

"Then there isn't enough time."

"What are you going to do to him, Cliff?"

"Now I go around doing things to people. What next?"

She stood up and walked woodenly back up the slope. I heard Trumbull's shout and she waved without enthusiasm.

In a few moments he was ashore, towel and swim suit

in his hand. As I came up he said, "I say, Mr. Bartells! This *is* damn decent of you."

"He's a very decent sort," Melody said coldly. "Good old Cliff."

Furny threw his head back and laughed. "You see, my dear, now you will simply have to listen to what I have to say."

She was trembling with anger. "And you might convince me, Furny. This time."

"That *is* good news, old girl."

"Come on and have a drink and then we'll go swimming," I said.

"Delighted, old man."

Melody moved close enough to me to whisper a word to me that I was surprised to find she knew. Her eyes were like hot gray smoke and her shoulders were rigid with anger.

Trumbull chattered as we all drank. The sun was hot and the Martinis were strong. Once Melody had her anger under control she reacted the way I might have expected. Everything Furny said was devastatingly funny. I got the cold eye every time I opened my mouth. She even hunched across the sand until she was a lot closer to Furny than to me.

I gave her no sign of victory. Just a wide bland smile. Which, of course, made her even more furious than ever.

Then we sat with our backs turned to the palms like good little boys while Melody changed to the yellow two-piece suit in which I had first seen her. Next Furny and I changed. We all went swimming. Both of them were smooth and good at it. I could make just as good time as they did, but I raised more of a wake. And I stayed close to them. Very close.

"Get lost," Melody said to me.

"We've got to have a little private conversation, old man," Furny pleaded.

"Nothing's private on an island," I said. I stayed close. Finally Furny gave up and swam back in to shallow water. We all went up on the shore and stretched out in a neat little row. Melody in the middle.

They chattered away. I waited them out. When at last the sun's heat brought silence, I said, "Of course, Furny, you have to eliminate me too."

"What on earth is he talking about, darling?" Furny asked her.

"He has fits," she said acidly.

"It's funny how it starts, Furny," I said. "You killed Elizabeth and you learned how easy it is. You made a little profit, but not enough. So I've set up the next step for you. What could be neater? A nice little island where nobody can possibly see you."

He sat up and peered at me. "Have you gone absolutely crackers?"

"That lawyer of yours is no dummy. He's given you the pitch. All Melody has to do is go through the proper motions and that codicil is as dead as Aunt Elizabeth. It will be an excellent idea for you, Furny, if she never gets to Boston."

He made a face at Melody. "Could comic books have done this to him?"

"You're as cool as they come, Trumbull."

"The man talks like a cop," Furny said with mock astonishment.

I grinned over at him, across Melody's slim tanned body. "I am, friend, Deputy Chief of the Florence City police. That's why I invited you here. It seemed like a nice place to pick you up."

Furny yawned. "Old boy, you can talk nonsense until the cows come home. I'm going to take a nap. And when I wake up, I'm going to be hungry."

He lay back with his back toward Melody.

I saw the muscles of the brown arm and shoulder move and, like a fool, I didn't get it. But when I heard the snap of rubber, I woke up fast. I made a despairing lunge across Melody, trying to get at him. My fingers touched his damp back as he rolled away and then came up onto his knees.

"Now be good," he said in an odd tone.

The barrel of the little automatic glinted in the sun. On the sand lay the torn rubber sack that had protected the gun from the sea water when it nestled in the pouch of his snug swimming trunks.

"Furny!" Melody said. "What are . . ."

"Back off her, Bartells. Farther. Now sit facing me and hug your knees. Get beside him, Melly. About five feet away. That's right."

"What are you . . ."

"Melly, you are unspeakably dense. Kindly get it through that beautiful blonde skull that I'm going to kill you."

I felt dizzy with disappointment and dismay. The only thing I could think of was to save time for Melody, to get him talking.

"Did you plan to kill Elizabeth?"

He looked at me. "No. As a matter of fact, it was a rather stupid thing to do. I was in a sweat about money I owed. I had that quarrel with Melly and went home. I was afoot. Just by the greatest chance I met Elizabeth walking over to get me. She was quite excited. All the way back to her place she babbled about the people who had tied her up. I asked her why she hadn't phoned the police. She said she wanted to show me something and get my advice.

"I went up there with her. She unlocked the door. No one saw us. She had a coat on and she had rolled her pajama legs up to hide them. She had shut the safe again. She opened it and stood in front of it. I could see all that money. Money that I needed very badly. She was saying something about it being proof that Horace was in on it. I had been carrying a—sap, I believe you call them. I was afraid of thugs who might try to beat me up because of the bad check.

"Suddenly I knew what I had to do. As she started to turn I hit her as hard as I could. I took the money, took her coat off, and hung it up. I took her slippers off and put them under the bed and rolled down the pajama legs. I picked up the things they had tied her with and then I looked around very carefully. I took the paste ruby off the dresser. I couldn't see anything wrong with the picture. I let myself out, being careful not to leave prints. No one saw me leave. I tied the cords and things onto the sap and threw it out into the water, as far as I could."

I looked over at Melody. She was breathing harshly through her open mouth and her eyes did not waver from the small steady muzzle. It was a toy, but deadly as a cannon at that range.

He smiled brilliantly, flash of white teeth against the tan.

"But we *are* wasting time. All sorts of regrets, old girl. I'll tow you well out into the gulf."

As he lifted the automatic and aimed right between her eyes, she gave a strangled sound and tried to lunge into my arms. The gun made a little snapping sound, hardly louder than a cap pistol. She dropped face down, still reaching for me with the hand that had suddenly gone still.

I rolled out of that awkward position and leaped for him. A line of fire was drawn down the back of my shoulder and then my hand closed on his gun hand. He clubbed me with the other hand, but I got his wrist bent back until I could slide my hand down and rip the gun out of his fingers. I threw it blindly away, just as he wrenched free. He got to his feet first and kicked at my face. His naked foot brushed my cheek and I dived forward to catch the other ankle in my hands and pull it out from under him.

He went down on his back and I pinned him, astride him, my knees across his arms. I saw through redness, and then I couldn't see him. The sun was beating on me and I was sobbing. It was the weariness of my arms that finally halted me. Then my vision slowly cleared and I could see his unconscious face. Not a face any longer.

It was a red and meaningless thing, like a raw standing rib roast. A shard of the lower jaw bone, breathlessly white in the sun, protruded from his cheek. I thought he was dead. But breath bubbled in his throat. I climbed off him and looked at my darling, behind me on the sand.

I crawled to her on my knees, panting with weakness. I touched the gold and silver hair, still damp from the sea. I rolled her over onto her back, and she was as limp as a rag doll.

The eyes opened and this time they were the softest blue I had ever seen. They were vacant and wide and the knowledge slowly came back into them. Her mouth puckered up and her face screwed up. "My head hurts, Cliff. Gee, my head hurts."

What sense can you make when you laugh and cry at the same time? They don't see men cry. When they do, it scares them. And I was the one being comforted.

After a time she lay on her face and I gingerly parted the heavy hair. Near the roots it was clotted with blood. The gash wasn't deep. It had stopped bleeding.

She went and looked down at Furny for a long time. I expected her to wince or to be sick. She turned and stared at me calmly. "You did that when you thought he'd killed me, didn't you?" I nodded. Her fingers clawed into her bare thighs. "If he had killed you, I'd get a stone and I'd pound and pound and pound until there was no head at all." It was pure savage. She meant it. Given the chance, she'd do it.

"I didn't want to kill him. The law, in its own way, is more sadistic than any death like that. Let's get him into the shade."

He came out of it before the boat came. He tried to talk but we couldn't understand what he was trying to say. He seemed to be pleading and the one eye that wasn't swollen shut had a glitter of primitive alarm. The fine suave manner of Mr. Furness Trumbull was gone, showing that underneath he was a punk like any other. The court would undoubtedly fail to show premeditation. He'd be out again, someday. By then he'd probably be in his fifties—if he was lucky. For a man of his stamp, it would have been a kindness to kill him. When the ego went, the mind would probably go with it.

We made him as comfortable as we could. We sat a few dozen feet away from him and waited for the launch.

"You could have told me," she said.

"I'm not proud of myself."

"What's this police business? Are you serious?"

"Completely."

"We'll . . . have to talk about that, Cliff."

"Indeed we will."

At last the launch came and the man swallowed his smile when he saw what we had for him. When we tried to move Trumbull he fainted with the pain. The man had a tarp in the launch. We slid him onto that and lifted him in. After we got to the dock it took thirty-five minutes for the ambulance to arrive. The driver taped my scratched shoulder. I made my calls and Harry got there just after the ambulance did. He reassured the launch owner that I wasn't a dangerous maniac. He took Melody and me down for statements. We left the cold chicken and the beer with the launch man.

We had a belated lunch in town with Harry and then went out to his house. During lunch Harry and I talked about plans for the department. Melody maintained an ominous silence.

Angela was very shy and ill at ease with Melody. Melody, I could see, and I liked her for it, tried hard to put Angela at ease. The tiny living room was furnished with fat, shiny overstuffed furniture—the last thing you should own in Florida. It was dim and almost airless, despite the open windows.

The shop talk went on. At last Melody stepped into a break in the conversation. "Let's have a word from a rebellious minority," she said. "Me, I don't want to wheel laundry into the room, Cliff, but don't I come in on this? I thought we were set. This big deal of being the wife of a Florence City cop doesn't exactly intrigue me."

It fell into the silence like a stone. She felt it and blushed a little as Harry shifted uneasily in his chair. "I don't mean that it isn't a nice occupation," Melody said, making matters worse, "but we're not going to be in the sort of situation where you have to do that—sort of thing, Cliff."

I glared at her and she glared back.

Angela, surprisingly, raised her voice for the first time. "I s'pose you got just barr'ls a money, Miz Chance."

Melody gave her a startled look. "Uh—yes, I guess you'd call it that."

Angela straightened her shoulders. "Good-lookin' gal like you, with that money, kin git herself any number of poodle-dog men, lickin' around, he'pin' spend it, I'd say."

"Yes, but . . ."

Angela went inexorably on. "Now, you want a man that's a man, Cliff here's good as most, but honey, you won't get youself noplace tryin' to make a poodle-dog man outa him. Man's got things to do he has to do, and Harry always says Cliff is a good cop and right now Harry sorta needs him to he'p. You cart him off an' pretty soon neither a you got no respeck. No respeck a-tall. I'm pure talkin' too heavy, but on'y because Cliff has been our friend a long time."

She got up with stiff dignity and walked out of the room into the kitchen.

Melody looked over at me for a long time. She dropped her eyes. "A girl can learn something every day."

"So can I, Melly. Look. Three months here getting things lined up. Then I'll take four months off, if Harry says O.K., and see how much of your dough we can unload in four months. Then back on the job."

Melody stood up. I would have thought her completely subdued were it not for the pixie glint in her eyes, the glint that promised future defiance, future battles when the making up would be the best part of it.

"I guess that's something for you men to decide," she said softly. "I'll go out and see if I can help Angie."

ABOUT THE AUTHOR

JOHN D. MacDONALD, says *The New York Times,* "is a very good writer, not just a good 'mystery writer.'" His Travis McGee novels have established their hero as a modern-day Sam Spade and, along with MacDonald's more than 500 short stories and other bestselling novels—60 in all, including *Condominium*—have stamped their author as one of America's best all-round contemporary storytellers.

JOHN D. MacDONALD

The Travis McGee Series

Follow the quests of Travis McGee, amiable and incurable tilter at conformity, boat-bum Quixote, hopeless sucker for starving kittens, women in distress, and large, loose sums of money.

THE DEEP BLUE GOOD-BY	14176	$1.95
NIGHTMARE IN PINK	14097	$1.75
A PURPLE PLACE FOR DYING	14219	$1.95
THE QUICK RED FOX	14098	$1.75
A DEADLY SHADE OF GOLD	14221	$1.95
BRIGHT ORANGE FOR THE SHROUD	14243	$1.95
DARKER THAN AMBER	14162	$1.95
ONE FEARFUL YELLOW EYE	14146	$1.95
PALE GRAY FOR GUILT	14148	$1.95
THE GIRL IN THE PLAIN BROWN WRAPPER	14256	$1.95
DRESS HER IN INDIGO	14170	$1.95
THE LONG LAVENDER LOOK	13834	$1.95
A TAN AND SANDY SILENCE	14220	$1.95
THE SCARLET RUSE	13952	$1.95
THE TURQUOISE LAMENT	14200	$1.95
THE DREADFUL LEMON SKY	14148	$1.95
THE EMPTY COPPER SEA	14149	$2.25
THE GREEN RIPPER	14345	$2.50

Buy them at your local bookstore or use this handy coupon for ordering.

This offer expires 1 June 81   8999